T0115152

Black Roses

JENNIFER JO FAY

authorHOUSE®

AuthorHouse™
1663 Liberty Drive
Bloomington, IN 47403
www.authorhouse.com
Phone: 1-800-839-8640

First published by AuthorHouse 3/22/2011

ISBN: 978-1-4567-4992-7 (e)
ISBN: 978-1-4567-4993-4 (sc)

Library of Congress Control Number: 2011904561

Printed in the United States of America

\mathcal{I}t was a sunny afternoon in the middle of October. The town of South Haven was quiet for the moment. The black birds were perched on the telephone wire across the street from a pretty blue cape house. The yard was surrounded by a white picket fence. Some of the paint on the fence was chipping. The owner needed to have it repainted. A little gray squirrel scurried under the fence and ran up a nearby oak tree to hurry to safety. A black Porsche drove up to the cape house. A person got out of the car and opened up the mailbox. The stranger slipped some black roses in the mailbox. The person stepped into the car again and drove away quickly. Someone was about to receive an ominous message. The threat of death was lurking in the shadows of a beautiful day.

A robin with an orange belly flew down to the grass and searched for worms. It pranced about the yard. The grass was really green. It wasn't brown like some of the other yards. The owner needed to mow the grass. It was getting long. There were several large gardens near the fence. The owner had planted lots of perennials. There was an abundance of coneflowers, sweet peas and black-eyed susans a clump

of white daisies were grown near the porch. The number on the house was seven. Was it going to be an unlucky number? The porch was a large closed in veranda with lots of windows. The trim was painted a darker blue than the rest of the house. The shutters were also dark blue. On two of the windows on the ground floor there were some window boxes filled with impatiens and geraniums. The colors were magenta pink and a vivid luscious red. It was almost the color of cadmium.

The warm rays of the sun shined down on the gardens, warming the tender petals. There was a soft breeze that made them sway. The daisies became a tangled mass and then stopped moving a few minutes later. It was fifty degrees out. It was unusual weather for October. Would the weather change to match the dreariness of ivory black roses?

The robin disappeared from the grass and flew away. There was a worm dangling from its mouth. There was a baby bird somewhere that needed the nourishment. The worm's tragic life was almost at an end. Whoever lived inside the house was completely unaware of what would be the future.

Suddenly a mail truck drove up and down the street delivering mail. The blue cape had a mailbox at the end of the driveway. It had a picture of lilacs on the side of the mailbox. The owner bought it online and replaced the old mailbox. The old one had been hit with a baseball bat one evening.

The mail truck stopped at their mailbox. The postman opened it a put in the mail. It consisted of several catalogs, some bills and a large manila envelope. The mailbox got closed and the mailman drove away. The mailman looked back and hesitated. He had seen the black roses and wondered who had sent them. He wondered about the threat of death.

The large blue door of the cape opened and a woman

walked out. She had long curly blond hair, fair skin and baby blue eyes. She was five foot seven inches. She was wearing a navy blue oxford shirt and a tan skirt that ended below her knees. Her shoes were black flats. She wore a necklace that was filled with red hearts. It looked like an antique. Her fingernails were well manicured and painted a fancy pink color. It was the color of rose petals.

She stepped out of the porch and walked down the driveway. First she opened the door to her green Honda Oddessy. She grabbed a day old black coffee cup out of the car. The woman walked to her mailbox and retrieved her mail. She was startled by the black roses. Some of her mail was heavy. She walked back towards the porch. On the way she admired her coneflowers. Those were her favorites. Even though her hands were full, she managed to stop and clip a few pink roses from her nearby rose bush. She had planted many roses over the last few years. She had bought many of them with her Chase credit card. She had several different cards that were almost maxed out. She carried the cut roses inside. Later she was going to put them in a vase. She sat down in one of her green wicker rocking chairs. She had bought two of them for her porch. She had discovered them in a catalog. They were one hundred fifty dollars a piece. She loved them. There was also a little glass table to match. She desperately needed that too. The table was also one hundred fifty dollars. She also liked to shop at Marshalls. On an earlier visit to the store she had purchased a set of four poppy patterned tea cups. She also bought some yellow floral pillows for the wicker chairs.

Currently one of the tea cups was resting on the table. Hot chocolate was in the cup, but now it was lukewarm. The woman picked up the cup and went into her well stocked kitchen to heat it in her pink microwave. She threw out the black roses . She didn't want to be reminded of threats.

After a minute and twenty seconds, she retrieved the cup and went back to the porch. She sat down. She grabbed the roses and saw her wedge wood blue vase on the table. It still had some water in it from yesterday. Some daisies were bent and touching the table. Bent daisies. Was that the beginning of a beautiful poem? The woman liked to write poetry. Next to the vase was a blue leather-bound journal and a Paper mate ballpoint pen was resting in a pen holder. The holder was decoupage with old fashioned stamps of ballerinas. The stamps had been glued on. They were dated back to the nineteen seventies.

The woman was thirty years. She was absolutely beautiful. She was very slender. She put one rose in the vase. As she went to put the other one in she pricked her finger on the green thorn. A drop of blood appeared and it dripped. The woman gasped at the sight of blood. She remembered back to her childhood when her best friend, Lila dared her to cut her finger open. She hadn't wanted to do it. She didn't like the sight of blood. It made her think of dead people. That long ago day, her friend had grabbed a nearby knife and sliced her finger for her. She had screamed and fainted. Her friend had given her a Scooby doo band aid. That day they rubbed their bloodied fingers together and made a pact to be best friends forever.

The woman smiled at her remembrance. Her friend lived in Kingston. It was the next town over. They were still best friends. There was a secret that the woman kept from Lila. She chose not to tell her everything. She didn't want Lila knowing all about her. Some secrets were best kept hidden. Lila would be horrified if she knew about Sarah's secret life. She also wondered if she should hide the fact that she was receiving the black roses. They weren't the first ones. She felt afraid of what they meant.

The woman looked at her finger dripping. She stood and

went into the kitchen. She kept a box of band aids mixed in with her boxes of elbow noodles and other foods in her cupboard. She opened the box and pulled out a small band aid. She covered her finger. She went back to the porch and sat down again. She stuck the other rose in the vase. It tilted to the side like a melancholy rose. She thought of a famous black and white photograph by Andrez Kertaz. She remembered that she had a postcard of the picture.

The woman looked at the mail. She skimmed through the catalogs. One was an L.L. Bean catalog. Sometimes she ordered some of the outfits. She had ordered a woven white hammock from it last year. She had tied it to two of her birch trees. The hammock had come to two hundred dollars. She had used her Chase credit card. The other catalog was the Lakeside collection. There was a lot of cheap stuff in that one. She had purchased a New Moon throw with Edward and Bella on it. It kept her warm sometimes. Today she planned to throw out both catalogs. There was her Chase credit card bill, her gas bill and bills for two more credit cards. Her Chase credit card was at ten thousand dollars. The other two credit cards were at fifteen thousand dollars a piece. She had also done a lot of travelling on her cards. Ten years ago she started travelling. She loved it. She thought it was great to see new places. She would probably never get the chance to go again. She set her bills aside. She planned to pay them next week. She wished she could just throw her bills away and start fresh. She needed to stay away from the malls. Fate brought her there. She loved to shop. It was a bad habit. She wondered if she could change her life around. It wasn't that easy. There was conflict in her life. There were things that she thought she couldn't escape from. Secrets were buried in her brain. And now someone was out to get her.

Then she spied the manila envelope. It was staring her

in the face. Did she dare open it? She really didn't want to. Fate told her to open it. She was curious. It wasn't the first one. It had happenedthree other times. There was no return address. The mailman probably didn't put it in her mailbox. It was addressed in black lettering to Sarah Fisher. The person definitely didn't know her middle name was Marissa. She had an awful feeling she wasn't going to like what was inside the envelope. It was another reminder of what might come her way. She would be mortified.

Sarah took another sip of her hot chocolate. She cursed when she spilled some on her shirt. She was clumsy today. She grabbed a nearby towel and dabbed at her shirt. She hoped it wouldn't leave a stain. Sometimes she spilled raspberry jelly on her shirts and it left a stain. She liked jam on her English muffins.

She hesitated and picked up the envelope. It was a little bulky. Something other than paper was in it. Sarah opened the envelope and dumped the contents onto the table. There was a piece of paper with some black lettering on it. There was also a small box of chocolates and a black rose was resting on the tabletop. Sarah didn't like seeing the black rose. It sent frigid chills up her spine. She read the note. It was a poem.

Black roses linger on my mind.
For you my sweet are a black rose
awaiting my sharp knife. Soon my dear.
My black rose.

Sarah dropped the letter. It made her panic. The letter was the same as the other ones. She sat at the table the other times and each time she worried about who sent the letters. Where did they come from? What was the person thinking? Someone out there wanted blood on his knife. She just

assumed that it was a man. What if it was a woman? She really had no clue.

The three other letters had arrived last week on three different days. Sarah looked at the chocolates and reached for them. As much as she liked chocolate she had to throw them out. What if they were tampered with? They looked like they were filled with raspberry flavor. Sarah couldn't risk it. What if they were laced with poison? She didn't want to die at the hand of a killer. What a waste of good chocolate. Sarah liked to buy the bags of Lindt chocolate at Christmas. Sometimes she would devour the bag in one sitting. Her mother had loved chocolate also. She wished that her mother was still around. Life had changed.

Sarah looked at her fingernails. The paint was starting the chip. She should repaint her fingernails. Maybe she would paint them purple. Her nine year old niece, Beth liked purple. Beth enjoyed Friday night sleepovers at Aunt Sarah's house. It was usually pizza night. That was their favorite food. Tomorrow was Friday. She was going to pick up Beth in the afternoon. Sarah's sister, Judy was going to have a night out with a blind date named, Harry. It was her first date since her divorce. Judy had been divorced from her ex-husband, Henry for two months. Recently they had called each other and talked about getting back together. Sarah thought that would be good. Maybe they could start fresh and begin again. There was always the possibility of newfound love with each other.

The Friday night sleepovers were good therapy for Beth. Beth had a lot to deal with. She was being pulled by two strings. One was attached to Judy and the other was attached to Henry. Henry and Judy were always fighting and Beth was in the tragic center. It was like she was immersed in a blood bath of battering words. Once Beth caught Judy holding a black frying pan. She was ready to attack Henry

with it. She had chased Henry around the kitchen with it. Beth had cried out, "Don't hurt my daddy!"

Sarah read the poem again. She felt sickened by the poem. The other poems were tucked away in a drawer in her living room. It was hidden in her end table. She placed the fourth poem with the others. She sat on her rose patterned sofa. It had cost her nine hundred dollars. She loved it. She grabbed one of her coffee table books. It contained pictures of Audrey Hepburn. As she looked at the pictures, she couldn't keep her mind off the poems. Was someone out there watching her? How close were they to her house? The person obviously knew where she lived. Perhaps Sarah wasn't safe. Someone was messing with her. She was scared. She figured that she should take the poems to the police. Maybe they could find fingerprints. Tomorrow morning she would go to the police station with the poems, the chocolates and the black rose. Her life was being threatened and the police should know about it. She had never been stalked before. In her thirty years she had never been threatened. Now it was happening to her. She was going to be thirty one tomorrow. She wondered if the person knew when her birthday was. Maybe she would get a black card in the mail.

Sarah had no babies of her own. Her only sister had lucked out and had one. Beth was a special niece. Sarah doted on her. Sarah looked at the school picture of Beth. It was in the center of a jeweled frame. She had purchased the frame at Marshalls. Beth had straight red hair and was wearing a gingham jumper and a white turtleneck. She had freckles on her face. Beth inherited her red hair from Henry. Judy had blond hair like Sarah. Sarah and Judy looked a lot alike. Everywhere they went together, people could tell that they were sisters. Judy was two years younger than Sarah. Judy worked forty hours a week at Bed and Bath. She liked it. She worked days and she picked up Beth at a nearby

daycare. In two years she was going to let Beth stay home by herself after school. Right now she was too young. It wouldn't be right to leave her home alone. It would be bad parenting. Judy was a good mother.

Sarah thought back to ten years ago when she was twenty one. Sarah had been pregnant with her boyfriend, Justin Black's child. They had broken up after a two year relationship. He had black hair and brown eyes. He had been the most handsome man Sarah had ever met. Justin didn't give her an explanation as to why he broke up with her. She had loved Justin and couldn't believe that it was over. Two weeks after their break up she discovered that she was pregnant with his child. She went to his house in Kingston one evening to tell him the news. He said, "Are you sure it's mine?"

"Yes. You're the only man I've been with." "I want you to have an abortion!" "No. I can't do that." "Yes. You can. I forbid you to have the baby." "Justin. It's a human being!"

Justin reached for his checkbook. He wrote her a check for one thousand dollars. "Get the abortion and get out of my life. I mean it."

Sarah felt slapped in the face as Justin handed her the check. The check had the Anne Geddes babies on it. Sarah remembered walking out of his house with the check in her hand. She had gotten home to her one bedroom apartment. At the time she wasn't living at the cape. The cape was where her parents had lived. She had stared at the check for hours. She had wanted to burn it up. At the time she was facing becoming a single mother. It scared her. She didn't know if she could do it. A few days later, she cashed the check and made an appointment to have an abortion.

A week later she had been lying on a hospital bed. She was wearing one of the blue hospital gowns. The baby was gone and she had been crying. Motherhood was no longer

hers to hold. The loss was painful. There would always be that loss. Sarah had cried all night long for the loss of her baby. She was going to call her Samantha Jean Black. If it had been a boy she was going to name him Jeremy Lewis Black. Now the names had blown away in the silent wind. She cried for Justin. She had wanted him to make love to her again. Their sex had been great. Soft and gentle. She loved him deeply and the hurtful wound needed time to heal. At the time she had her mother to turn to. That had vanished with a tragic accident. Her parents had been killed a year ago in a tragic accident. A drunk driver had killed them. Sarah and Judy had been devastated. After a little bit, Sarah decided to move into her parent's home. It seemed to be the right thing to do. She still missed Justin too. The hurtful feelings finally sifted away into nothing.

Now was the present day. That had been ten years ago. Sarah had healed somewhat. She still had the little pink outfit in a white box. It was tucked away under her bed. She had purchased the item before she had confronted Justin. Now it waited for little Beth to have a baby. Or maybe her friend, Lila would have one. Lila had been married for two years and was pregnant with her first baby. She and Sarah had gotten together last week. That was before those eerie black roses started arriving.

Since Justin, Sarah hadn't met anyone that she could have settled down with. There had been lots of men in her life, but there was nobody special to fill the loss of Justin. Who could have sent her the creepy poems and roses? She tried to think about who she knew. It could be someone she knew or it could be a complete stranger. It killed her that she didn't know. Her mind was seriously worried.

She sat on her sofa and studied Audrey Hepburn. She liked the old fashioned actresses. She also liked the style of Katherine Hepburn. Sometimes she would play her

old movies. She had a big collection. She put those on her credit cards too. She also liked romance books. She liked the harlequins.

Suddenly Sarah stood from the sofa. She felt dirty from digging around the garden and now she was thoroughly horrified by the roses. First she walked to the porch, retrieved the poppy cup from the porch and put it in her kitchen sink. Later she would do the dishes. She didn't do them every day because it was just her living there. She didn't make a lot of dishes. She walked up the beige carpeted stairs to her bathroom. Along the stairway she had hanging on the wall several Renoir reproductions in lovely gold frames. She had spent a lot on getting them framed. That went on her credit card also.

She undressed and let her clothing drop to the floor. She let her skimpy black panties fall around her ankles. She stepped out of them. Then she unhooked her black bra. Sometimes she wondered why she liked the color black. There seemed to be something erotic about sweet black satin things. She liked having a sexy body. Justin's loss. She hoped she would eventually find somebody new. Judy was always telling her it would happen when she least expected it. She wondered when. Would something happen to change things for the worse? She thought about her front door. She didn't have it locked. She thought about the movie, Psycho. She didn't want to see a knife while she was in the shower.

She studied herself in the large oval mirror. The frame was a silver color and had embossed hearts on it. She had purchased the mirror from a catalog called Victorian Papers. It had cost her one hundred dollars. She slapped it on her credit card. She didn't like writing checks, but she had to pay back her cards. Maybe she could disappear and leave them behind. She would miss Judy and Beth.

Sarah got a pink comb and combed through her curls.

She looked at her breasts. She was a D-cup. They were large and round and her brown tits were big. She had a hickey on her lower neck. She couldn't remember getting that. Where did that come from? She felt embarrassed. She stepped into the hot steamy shower and washed her body with her rose scented soap. She smelled of sweet rose. Sweet roses. There was another good poem in the making. She would write about them later. She loved to write. She thought that everyone needed a hobby. That was hers.

When she stepped out she toweled off with a pink towel and walked into her bedroom. Her nude body was absolutely beautiful. No flaws. Her bedroom walls were pink. She walked over to her vanity table and looked at herself in the mirror. She liked her boobs. Her pubic hair was nice and squeaky clean. She opened her lingerie drawer and pulled out a red thong. It was made of strawberry licorice. Sweet. Tasty strawberries. She put on a few red tassels that just covered her nipples. She retrieved a tight wrap-a-round black dress from her large closet and put it on her body. She studied her abundance of high heeled shoes and decided on wearing a pair of red stilettos. She was ready. She looked at her clock. It was approaching six pm. It was early but she was ready to go out.

She looked at the picture of her parents. She felt guilty. She was going to do something that would put a frown on her mother's face. But that didn't matter now. Her parents were dead. There had been a little money from their parents. It was only two thousand dollars for each sister. It wasn't enough to pay off her credit cards. She was in a lot of debt. Judy kept asking her about her job. She had told Judy that she worked nights at a restaurant four towns away. She never told Judy where it was. Sometimes Judy questioned her about it. Sarah was embarrassed and pretended that she

didn't want to tell Judy about it. She didn't want Judy to know her dirty secret.

The night was still early. Sarah went to her living room and sat in her pink lazy boy chair. She read her harlequin for about three hours. She stopped reading at seven pm and ate a frozen dinner. She didn't always like to cook. She did enjoy baking cookies. Her mother used to make really good peanut butter cookies. She really missed her mother and father. There were many times that Sarah wished she could call her mom and talk to her. She used to cry to her about Justin. She was jealous of Judy's daughter. She really had wanted one of her own. She was really jealous of Judy. She did everything right. Judy was a really good girl. Sarah was always getting into trouble. Judy always had everything just right. Everything except for her divorce. That was messed up. Sarah never told her mother about all her credit cards. She didn't want her to worry. She loved the old pictures of her parents. Her mother had been beautiful and her father had been a really nice man. They had a beautiful relationship. Now it was wasted on a tragic death. Judy and Sarah never got over the death of their parents. Judy wore nothing but black for a month. Sarah tried not to talk about them. She didn't want to remember the pain. Her parents never discovered Sarah's secret. Sarah didn't want them knowing.

At nine pm Sarah set down her book and put her rose bookmark in it. Love's Sweetest Temptation was the title of the book. It was really good. It was mostly romance with a little touch of mystery to it. After she was done with it she was going to pass it on to Judy. Judy liked books by James Patterson and Ruth Rendell. Once in a while she read Sarah's harlequins.

Sarah grabbed her Gucci purse and her car keys. She locked the house and then got into her van and drove into downtown South Haven. It was dark and there wasn't many street lights on. Sarah parked her van and walked a few blocks up the street. She stepped into a bar. It was called Tangoes. There was a lot of smoke and a lot of men sitting around drinking beer. It was an underground strip club. The men could touch the women. In a regular strip club the men weren't allowed to touch the women. They could only have a lap dance. The strippers could rub their bodies on the men but they couldn't touch them. They could toss their tips on the stage into a bucket. Here everything was illegal. They got away with touching the strippers. Because of this the bar was always packed.

As Sarah stepped into the bar she heard someone holler her name. "Sarah, get in that dressing room. You're on in twenty minutes," said Benny. He had black hair and wore an earring in his ear. He wore a black tee shirt and jeans with holes in them. He had on dirty sneakers. He had lots of big muscles. He used to be a bouncer. Everyone listened to Benny. He was the authority. Sarah was afraid of what he could do. Benny had a tall glass of beer in his hands. He had drunk half of it. He took a puff from his cigarette and dabbed it in an ashtray. There were a lot of men at the tables. Girls with red bathing suits were waiting on them and getting them their beers. They weren't strippers but were waitresses. Benny liked all the women to dress skimpy.

Sarah passed Benny and went into the dressing room. She seated herself at a plush chair and began to apply some makeup to her cheeks. The room was painted a sea green color. Then suddenly she looked at the dresser table. There were one dozen black roses in a blue vase. A note was attached. It was a small piece of white paper. Sarah opened it. Inside in black lettering it said, Soon my black rose.

Sarah dropped it on the floor. Had the person followed her here? Who was it? The person was tampering with her life. Was the stranger fucking with her? Sarah felt a wave of horror rush over her. She picked the note off the floor and tucked it into her purse. She would go to the cops first thing tomorrow. This time there were no chocolates to throw out. She wondered if the person was in the audience. Soon twenty minutes ticked by and she was to be on stage. For the past few evenings there was also a police officer in the audience. Sarah wondered about that. She wondered if Benny was going to get in trouble. She hoped so. She thought that he would deserve it. Benny had done some not very nice things to Sarah.

She left her jittered nerves in the dressing room and danced and pranced her way onto the stage. She grabbed a microphone and started singing in a sultry voice. She was a good singer. She inherited her voice from her mother. Sarah used to sing all the time when she was younger. There were videotapes of her singing.

Sarah sang for her audience. After ten minutes of singing she quickly flung off her dress. It landed on the floor nearby. Sarah started dancing erotically. She could hear the men whistling and hollering. She had nothing on except her licorice underwear. She was beginning to sweat into them. She continued to dance. She was very good at it. She had been practicing for years. She danced near a pole and slid her body around it and arched her back. She felt dirty and sexy at the same time. Her red tassels were flapping around as she danced. Some of the other strippers were dancing also. She slid to the edge of the stage and did a slow split. She lifted up her legs erotically and hopped off the stage into the audience. One man was a few feet away from her. He moved towards her and slowly stuck a ten dollar bill in her thong. He touched her pussy. He had gray hair and a full mustache.

He was chunky and smelled of beer and cigarettes. Sarah danced for him and rubbed her body against him. His hands held her waist as she straddled him. His hands groped for her breasts. He pushed his face between her breasts and tongued her. He pulled at her tassels and said, "Give me some pussy cream, sugar honey." He looked at her again and rested his hands on her butt. He put some more money in her g-string. "I want to see you after the show. My name is Teddy."

Sarah waved a kiss towards him and got off his lap. She then danced her way to several other men. She got more money in her g-string. One guy pulled her close and slipped her hand in his pants. "Feel that? I'm horny for you." After letting ten to fifteen other guys feel her body and give her money she danced her way back on the stage. She continued to dance erotically for them. She felt naughty as she slid her body around the pole. The men loved it. It was their primal instinct to look at the naked women. She was glad she never saw her sister walk in. What would she think?

Much later she and the other strippers left the stage. Sarah went back into the dressing room. She counted the tips. She accumulated one hundred and fifty bucks. That was good money.

Benny came in a looked at Sarah. He grabbed her money and pocketed half of it. He stuffed the money in his pants. Sarah still hadn't put her dress back on. She was sitting cross legged in the chair. Benny pushed her onto the floor. He pulled down his pants and got down on her. He violently ripped off her tassels and sucked her tits. He cupped her breasts in his burly hands. Then he bit at her nipples. She screamed. She didn't like it. But she was afraid of Benny. Benny slid his hands down to her thong and stuck his hand into her vagina. He plunged his big penis into her vagina and fucked her really hard. She felt wet and sticky after he

pulled out. "Teddy is waiting for you upstairs in room seven. Don't keep him waiting. Make me some good money." He left the room. She hated him raping her but she didn't dare do anything about it. After all, she was also his prostitute. She had to do what he said.

Sarah put on her dress and straightened herself up. She walked out of the dressing room and went upstairs. The stairs were covered with red carpeting. She wondered about Benny. Could he have sent her the flowers? She didn't know. Benny was her pimp. Why would he send her threatening notes? She slowly pulled open the door to room number seven. She saw Teddy sitting on the bed. The comforter was a malachite green and the walls of the room were painted crimson red. There were a few lamps on some of the tables.

"Come sit by me, Sarah." Sarah obeyed and sat next to Teddy. Teddy began to put his hands on her. She wondered why he knew her name. She hadn't even seen him before tonight. She looked at the nearby desk. She saw some money resting on it. There were five one hundred dollar bills with Ben Franklin on it. "Is that my money?"

"Want to do tricks for me? If you're good to Teddy, I'll give you extra." Sarah looked at him and licked her lips.

His salt and pepper hair and sideburns told her that he was probably older. His mustache looked like it had handlebars. Teddy wore a white oxford shirt and dress pants. His fancy shoes were brown. He wore a paisley tie. He looked like he came from good money. Maybe she could get him to pay her more money. That happened sometimes. Benny didn't know about it.

"How old are you? You look old enough to be my father. Are you going to be able to get it up? I hear it's harder to get your penis hard when you get older. Maybe that's an old wives tale."

"I'm fifty one, Sarah. My penis is already hard for you."

"How do you know my name?"

"I study up on you girls. Benny said you were one of the best. So how about you take off that skimpy black dress you're wearing and show daddy your pussy. I want to feel you come."

Sarah stood up from the bed. She looked at the yellow vase that was on the nightstand. It contained a bouquet of silk flowers. The blinds were wide open so anyone could see in. Luckily being on the second floor nobody could really see upstairs unless if Sarah went to the window. Benny had five prostitutes working for him.

Sarah looked at the clock on the nightstand. It was one am. She would have rather been home to watch True Blood or the Vampire Diaries. However, she did like the extra money she got. The pay was good. She just had to get used to obeying Benny and doing what the johns wanted her to do. Selling her body helped her pay her bills.

She undid her dress and let it slide to the floor around her stilettos. She stepped away from it. She had put on her tassels. They dangled from her nipples. Her edible underwear was riding up her crotch. She wanted him to eat her. A part of her liked being a bad girl. She thought of Judy and felt her face turn red. Judy never wore edible underwear. In fact, she had granny underwear from her pregnancy days.

Teddy said, "Dance for me, sugar. I want my private show." Sarah did as she was told. She began to erotically dance and sway her hips. She stepped closer to Teddy and began to undress him. She undid all the little buttons on his shirt. It fell behind his back and landed on the bed. She then proceeded to unzip his pants. She stripped him down to his jalapeno patterned boxers and he was wearing a Calvin Klein undershirt. He had hairy legs. When she

slid his undershirt over his head she discovered that he had a chest like an ape.

"Lie on the bed for me, sugar. I'm going to want to fuck you hard. I want to lick your pussy cream, but first I want to eat up your underwear, sugar peach." Sarah laid herself down on the bed. She watched Teddy remove his boxers. Teddy pressed his body against Sarah. His tongue licked every inch of her breasts. He plucked off her tassels and fiercely licked her tits. His tongue grazed them ferociously. Then his teeth bit down upon her tits. She cried as he bit them. Then he licked them some more. His lips and tongue slithered down her abdomen and slowly approached her pelvic region. Teddy began to chew at her licorice underwear. Sarah felt her body arch to his lips as he chewed vigorously. He in tune licked her pussy as he chewed. Teddy could smell the scent of her rose soap as he licked her. Then his tongue probed her vagina and he chewed and licked deeper. His tongue plunged in deep. Deep into the abyss.

"Orgasm for me, sugar peach." Sarah cried as he licked her fiercely. It was as if he was a crazed tiger and she was his piece of London broil. She quickly climaxed for him and he devoured. "I love your cream, sugar peach." Sarah moaned in ravenous ecstasy. She was hot for more.

Teddy then thrust his dick into her and he pushed in hard. He slapped her breasts and beat her senseless as he exploded into her. Twenty minutes of hard sex hurt her body, but she obeyed Teddy. His dick pressed harder and rougher into her vagina. She thought she would start to bleed because he was so rough. Then his tongue licked up and down her abdomen and exploded into her vagina again. He licked her clitoris until she cried out. "Give me your pussy cream again, sugar peach." His big fingers massaged her pubic hair. He chewed his way through the rest of her edible underwear. He ate her cream as she climaxed for him.

"Say my name, sugar peach. Scream out fuck. Say fuck me hard!"

"Fuck! Fuck! Fuck me hard, Teddy!"

Teddy penetrated her vagina again with his rock hard penis. Then he arched his back and fucked her as hard as he could. He rammed his rod into her. Teddy was sweating as he collapsed against her naked body. He chewed at her tits again. He never once kissed her lips. She was glad that he didn't. It wasn't about sweet lovemaking. It was pure hard sex and yummy cream.

Sarah had an orgasm again and he devoured her cream. It felt good in a way. Sarah liked her job. She screamed and moaned for Teddy. It was the life that she was used to. Yet, lately she was beginning to wonder if she could change her ways.

"Pussy, pussy, pussy. I love your pussy, sugar peach." He licked at her as if he was a cat licking her milk. Teddy was a man who truly loved good pussy. Benny was true to his word. Sarah was hot to trot and gave good blow jobs. She really fulfilled his needs.

Suddenly the time was up. Sarah got up and put on her black dress and her stilettos. Teddy moved towards her and slid his hands up to her vagina. She was startled.

"Hey! Time's up. We're all done."

"Not until Teddy says so."

"No. Time's up. I'm going to collect my money now." Sarah grabbed the five hundred dollars and tucked it into her dress.

Teddy pushed her on the bed, pushed up her dress and fucked her hard again. She lashed out and hollered, "Time's up, asshole."

"No it isn't, you whore." Sarah fought him off her, but he was too strong. He thrust his penis into her hard. After

fifteen minutes, he got up and let her fix her dress. "Asshole." She had to put up with him. It was all part of the job.

"Hey, be good to me. I plan to pay for your services again tomorrow. I want more of your cream."

Sarah left him in the room. She went downstairs. Benny was in the office. "How much did you get?"

"Five hundred."

"Give me two hundred of it." She reluctantly handed it over. She didn't like having to give him so much. She left the room before he could approach her and rape her. It was rape. She didn't like him fucking her, but she was afraid of him. He had a few thugs working for him. He was a little like the mafia. She remembered what they did to Louisa. She didn't want that to happen.

She walked outside the bar and went the two blocks to her van. Her vagina was hurting. She slowly got into the car and locked the door. She turned on her headlights and looked at the dashboard. There was another black rose resting near her windshield wipers. She stepped out and retrieved the rose. She was careful not to prick herself on the thorn. There was a note with it. She read the note. It said *sinner. I crave your blood on my knife.* Sarah glanced near her car. There was nobody else in the area. The night was silent. The person had come near when she wasn't looking. Sarah was scared. The person evidently knew that she had been dancing in the bar. He or she knew what Sarah did for a living and they thought that she was sinning.

Sarah didn't feel that way. The money was good. If it meant that she had to perform tricks for it, so be it. She performed about five nights a week. Tomorrow was Friday. It was her night off and she planned to have some quality time with Beth. She would pretend to be a normal girl and have some fun. She hoped that Beth would grow up to be a good girl. She didn't want her following in her footsteps. Beth was so innocent. Sarah was glad that Judy and Henry were going to try to make things work. That was really important. Sarah had wished that she and Justin could have reunited and worked things out. Maybe her life would have been different. Sarah couldn't change anything about that. It was all in the past. Some things just couldn't be changed. Maybe Sarah was a stripper and a prostitute for a reason. It definitely hardened her. It made her tough. She wasn't the sweet innocent woman that Judy thought she was.

The stranger walked up the stairs of the bar. The person watched Sarah leave and walked into the bar after she left. The bar was empty but the light was still on upstairs. Teddy hadn't left yet.

The stranger had watched Sarah dancing that evening. The stranger loved how she slid her body around that pole. The stranger watched and waited. The stranger wanted to play with her for a little while. Yet, for some reason the stranger loved her.

The stranger craved her blood. The person wanted her sinner's blood on a knife. The stranger watched her dance erotically. The stranger kept looking at her large breasts. The stranger wanted to cut them up. The stranger wanted to etch the word sinner on her beautiful body.

The stranger stopped at the top of the stairs. The person looked at the number seven on the door. Then the stranger turned the brown doorknob and opened the door.

The stranger saw Teddy standing by the bed. He was fully dressed and was about to leave the room.

The stranger pulled out a 9mm gun and shot Teddy in the head. Teddy fell back against the bed and his blood splattered on the bedspread and the floor. Teddy was dead instantly. The stranger put on latex gloves and stepped closer to Teddy. The stranger began to undress Teddy. The stranger left him naked in the room. The stranger liked his victims exposed. The stranger bagged Teddy's clothing and left the room. The door was closed. The stranger left the bar and walked across the street to the black Porsche and stepped inside. The stranger drove to a house in South Haven.

Sarah looked at the clock in her car. It was two am. She left Teddy just a few minutes ago. She was on her way home. She felt the aftermath of an orgasm. Her vagina was still swollen from Teddy. She thought of the note. She wasn't a sinner. She thought of Benny fucking her hard. It was clearly rape. She wondered if she should go to the cops about it. Then she thought of what Benny might do to her and she refrained from doing so.

Sarah got into her driveway, locked her van and unlocked her house. She walked into her kitchen and poured a glass of milk. She gulped it down and set the glass in the sink. She walked up her stairs to the bedroom. She pulled out a flannel nightgown with flowers on it. She slipped her body under the covers and fell asleep. When she was away from her secret life she liked to dress normal. She felt comfortable. She kind of led a double life. Yet, now she seemed to have somehow put herself in a dangerous position. She wasn't going to know how to get herself out of it. Things were coming.

The next morning Sarah woke up. It was nine o'clock in the morning. She was still a little groggy. She still had the memory of Teddy licking her vagina to hell and back. It felt good. She wondered if she would see him again on Saturday night. Sometimes older men were irresistible.

She searched her closet for a red sweater and a pair of Jordache blue jeans. She showered and dressed. She went to her kitchen and started to brew a pot of coffee. She filled the filter with Folger's coffee grounds. She opened up a box of Dunkin Donuts. She ate a raspberry filled donut. She thought of Teddy's tongue in her vagina. What if her vagina was filled with raspberry filling? She ate the donut and thought of Teddy forcing himself on her. She hadn't liked that. She had been off the clock. He had only paid her for an hour. His time had run out.

When she was done with the donut she went out to the porch and sat at her wicker chair. She picked up her journal and started to write some poetry. She liked to write when she had days to herself. She wrote romantic poetry. Suddenly she began to think of Justin. She wished she had someone to settle down with. She hadn't seen Justin in years. He was probably married with a few kids by now. Sarah wrote a poem and called it Sweet Scented Petunias. Maybe someday her Mr. Right would waltz into her life and change it. She liked to dream about things like that. It would make Judy happy.

Looking at the white clock on her table, she went into the living room and gathered the notes from the creep. She put on her blue wool dress coat, grabbed her keys and locked the door. She stepped into her van and started the ignition. She headed for the police station. It was located in downtown South Haven. She lived in a nice little neighborhood. South Haven also was a little like living in the country. There was a wooded forest in South Haven and there was a small lake

near the forest. Downtown South Haven was where all the shops were.

Once she arrived at the police station, she parked her car in the parking lot, got out of her car and went inside the station. The walls inside were a lemon yellow color. She saw a police officer at the counter. He was drinking a cup of coffee.

"Hi. My name is Sarah Fisher. Since last week I've been getting creepy messages in the mail along with chocolates and black roses. Someone is sticking them on my car also. The person knows where I work too. I don't know who it is, but I'm afraid that the person wants to hurt me."

"Do you have the evidence with you?"

"Yes. Here they are. Maybe you can find some fingerprints on them. Maybe the person was careless."

"I'll take them to our lab. We'll find out in a few days if there is anything on it. My name is Officer George Trent. Here's my card. Call me is the person sends you anything again."

"Thank-you."

Officer George Trent had short blond hair and blue eyes. He was muscular and was of medium weight. He was wearing a blue blazer and a yellow shirt. He also wore blue jeans. He looked like he was five foot seven inches. He seemed nice. She hoped he would find some fingerprints that would lead them to the creep. She wanted the stranger behind bars and away from her. She wanted the threatening letters to stop. The stranger wasn't going to get her blood on a knife. Not if she could help it. She was a strong woman. She vowed that she would never be a damsel in distress. Yet, the thought of being rescued by a charming man who was savagely handsome seemed like a nice dream. Sometimes she dreamed of that kind of thing. Usually nothing bad ever happened to her in her dreams. She always got saved.

The man in her dreams usually looked like Fabio. Rippling muscles and raw sweat. Yum. Sometimes her deep dark mind took her to exotic places where several men devoured her and they were her slaves of desire. She liked an erotic man. Sometimes she dreamed of a man chasing her and devouring her with flaming passion. That's what dreams were made of. She left Officer Trent and wandered away. She made sure she tucked his card in a safe place.

That morning Benny left his apartment and walked the two blocks to Tangoes. He was wearing a red long sleeve tee shirt underneath a brown leather jacket. His blue jeans had holes in them. He wore a big pair of L.L. Bean boots. He watched his shadow as he walked along the sidewalk. It was sunny out but the air was really cold. It was a prelude to winter. Once at Tangoes, he fumbled with the keys, let himself in and began to clean up the bar. Then he went into his office and sat at his black desk. The walls in the office were painted red. The whole bar was red like the color of blood. Fifteen minutes later Benny's maid, Ursula Jenkins poked her head into the office. She was an older woman with gray hair. She was wearing a blue shirt underneath a wool black sweater. She also wore a pair of blue jeans. She had on brown clogs. Benny liked Ursula. She was always prompt. She did a thorough cleanup job. She usually vacuumed the carpets in the bar and cleaned the rooms upstairs. There were three bedrooms on the second floor. Usually when all the rooms were occupied with the prostitutes, the other's that didn't have a room performed their sexual acts in the hallways. At least they weren't on the streets. Benny paid her one hundred bucks a week to clean. She came in one or two days to clean. She went about her vacuuming and when she was done she grabbed some cleaning supplies and headed upstairs. Ten minutes later Benny heard her scream. He ran up the stairs to see what had happened. He saw the door number seven was open and the light from the sun was seeping into the hallway. He walked into the room and felt like vomiting. Teddy was extremely dead and naked. He couldn't believe his eyes. Suddenly he thought of Sarah. She had been the last person to see him alive at 2am. Was she capable of murder. Benny thought about Sarah as a killer for a moment and then shoved the thoughts aside.

She was his prostitute. He didn't want to think of her as a killer. He and Ursula left the room and went downstairs. Benny picked up the black phone and called the cops in South Haven.

Benny waited at the bar. He made a pot of Chock full of nuts coffee. He thought about the dead man. This was going to be bad for business. What the hell did Sarah do to him? He thought he knew his girls. He wondered if he was going to have his thugs pay a visit to Sarah's house. He didn't want bad business. Susie Lockhart was due into the bar at 9pm. There would be a john waiting for her after hours. Would there be another death on their hands? Benny didn't want to think about it. Yet, deep down in his secret mind he knew something. He didn't want to tell anyone.

Ursula sat at a nearby table with her head in her hands. "What is this world coming to? I've never seen someone dead before. Whoever killed that guy has a morbid soul. To strip him of his clothing is creepy."

Ten minutes later, the cops arrived and pulled up their cop car across from Tangoes. Officer George Trent and his partner, Officer Larry May walked into the bar. Officer May had a buzz cut. He was six foot and two inches and all muscle. He worked out at a local gym in the evenings. He had a gold earring in his nose. Officer May was wearing a green trench coat over a blue oxford shirt and a pair of Calvin Klein blue jeans. He wore black dress shoes on his feet. The two officers looked at Benny. "I'm Officer George Trent and this is Officer Larry May. So where is the body?"

"He's upstairs in room number seven." Benny drank his black coffee and studied the officers.

"Who found him?" asked George.

"I did," Ursula said. "I was going into the room to clean it and I found him there on the bed. dead. It was awful. It's the most horrible thing I have ever seen." Her face was pale and shocked.

"About what time did you find him?"

"It was ten thirty. I went vacuumed first downstairs and

then went straight upstairs to room seven. I'm going to guess that he was there all night."

"What time did you close Tangoes?" Larry asked Benny. Benny had just finished his coffee and was pouring himself another cup.

"I closed the bar at one am. I was here until 2:10am. Teddy had paid for Sarah's services from one am until two am."

"Who's Sarah?" asked Larry.

"Sarah Fisher is one of my girls. She's one of my five strippers. She's also a prostitute. I run Tangoes. "

"I hear you run an underground strip club. You know that it's illegal. We could press charges."

"How about you go take a look at the john. Sarah was the last one to see him alive. Maybe you should be talking to her." Benny looked disgusted. His thoughts turned to Sarah. He was so angry, he decided he would rape her hard next time he saw her. She deserved it. The filthy whore.

George and Larry walked upstairs. They went into the room and saw Teddy lying naked on the bed. Teddy had a bullet in his forehead. Larry set up some yellow crime scene tape. It was officially a crime scene. They walked around the room and began to dust for fingerprints. The covers on the bed were messed up. There was Teddy's crimson blood all over the bed. It was also splattered on the floor. A single black rose was resting near Teddy's stomach. George looked around the room for a sign of Teddy's clothing, but found absolutely nothing. The killer had confiscated it. The murderer had stripped him of his identity. There was also no trace of a wallet anywhere.

A few minutes later the forensics team came in and started investigating. They started checking for fingerprints, taking photographs and looking for trace evidence. Larry found a piece of red licorice on the bed near Teddy's head.

He picked it up with gloved hands and put it in a plastic baggie. He found several blond hairs on the covers and bagged them also. The hairs were long. Larry wondered if they belonged to the prostitute.

George figured out that Teddy had been dead since two am or somewhere around that timeframe. There were no footprints anywhere. The blinds were closed. Had the murderer closed the blinds? After one hour, George and Larry went back downstairs. A little while later the forensics team would put Teddy in a black bag and bring him to the funeral home.

George found Benny in his office. "What was the john's name? What do you know about him?"

"His name was Teddy Barrington. He lived in South Haven. He leaves behind a wife and two kids."

"Did he come here often?"

"Last night was the first night. Sarah had him for an hour. She gets five hundred dollars and I pocket two hundred."

"Easy money for you. Were you still here when Sarah left?"

"Yes. I locked up ten minutes after she left. I never went upstairs." Benny said. "I live in an apartment a few blocks away. I live on Torrensen Street."

"So maybe he was murdered between two am and two ten. Did you hear anyone come into the bar?" He paused and then decided that they needed an answer. He thought quick.

"No. I had the radio on. I was listening to Def Leopard. That was the last song before I turned It off and headed home. When I got home I went straight to bed. Well, after a gin and tonic."

"Did you notice anything unusual as you were locking up?"

"No. I locked up and got in my BMW and left. It was cold last night. Sometimes I walk to work."

"Can you give me your phone number in case we need to ask you more questions?"

"Sure." Benny grabbed a piece of yellow sticky note paper that was on his desk and jotted down his number for George. He handed it to him. George thanked him and left the bar. Benny breathed a sigh of relief. He was glad that was over. Cops made him sweat. He didn't want to see his bar shut down. He had to play his cards right. He thought of Sarah and knew that he could shut her up like he did Lousia. Louisa was afraid of him now.

George and Larry drove back to the station and gave the evidence to the crime lab to process. Susan Gallagher was in the lab holding the evidence. She was the coroner. She was a slightly chunky five foot seven woman. She had black hair that was in the style of a bob cut. It stopped a little above her broad shoulders. She wore a long white lab coat with pockets over a red polo shirt and blue jeans. She was wearing mascara and pink blush on her cheeks. In her pierced ears were little sea shell earrings. George could smell her White Shoulders perfume.

"It should take a few hours to process and then I'll have the results." Susan looked at George. She flirted with him. They had been dating each other for the last three months. He hadn't wanted to get involved with someone at work, but Susan was too sexy and charismatic.

"Thank-you, Susan. What time do you get off work?"

"Around six pm. I need to be at the funeral home later to do the autopsy on Teddy Barrington. Why?"

"Will you be hungry?"

"Sure."

"How about going to the Thirsty Turtle for some appetizers and some beers?"

"That sounds good. Sure. By then I will have built up an appetite."

Just then George's cell phone rang. "Hello? I'll be right there, bye."

George looked for Larry and found him in his office. "There's been a drug bust on Severence Street. We're wanted there."

They left again and Susan got to work on the red licorice and the hairs. Susan was very good at her work. She was also very attractive and single. She really had the smoldering passion for George. He was her McDreamy.

It was one pm. Sarah was on her way to pick up Beth. Judy lived on Maple Street in South Haven. She arrived at Beth's house. Judy lived in a yellow ranch house. Judy's red car was in the driveway. Judy's ex-husband, Henry lived in Kingston. Sarah let herself in and found Beth sitting in the living room on a green sofa. The walls were a peach color and Judy had several landscape pictures on the walls. There was also a bunch of Beth's artwork taped to the walls. Beth was busy watching Spongebob Squarepants. "My favorite character is Patrick," Sarah told Beth.

"I like Sandy Cheeks. She's really funny." Beth's red hair was tied back with an orange bow. She was wearing a pink striped shirt and a pair of bell bottom blue jeans. There were pink flowers embroidered at the bottom of the pants. She was also wearing pink and white sneakers. They were a pair of Sketchers.

"Where is your mom?"

"She's upstairs washing her hair. She'll be down in a few minutes."

Sarah waited with Beth. They finished an episode of Spongebob Squarepants. After ten minutes, Judy came downstairs with a pink towel wrapped around her head. She had a purple phone in her hand. "Henry, I told you before I don't like it when you let Beth stay up until eleven at night. She has school the next day. You also feed her too many ring dings. Junk food, Henry. She'll rot her teeth. Try to be a better parent, for Christ sake. These are the things we need to work on when we get back together. Are we still on for next Thursday. It will be nice for all three of us to be together again. I love you and I want to have this work. Bye." Judy set the phone down on the kitchen counter.

"I'm glad you're getting back together."

"Me too. I miss him. I suppose I'll still go on that date, but I tell him I just want to be friends." Judy undid her

towel and let her wet blond hair fall to her shoulders. She was wearing a blue cashmere sweater and a long black skirt. She work black sweater tights and black pumps. Judy tapped her fingernails on the counter. "Beth might be tired tonight. Henry had her last night and there was no set bedtime. He spoils her rotten. He doesn't act like a dad. He lets her eat lots of junk food and he lets her sleep in her blue jeans. He leaves his damn gun out In plain sight. Doesn't he realize Beth could grab it and hurt herself? She's only nine. Next he'll probably teach her how to hunt deer with him. Good lord. We've got a lot of hard work ahead of us. But if our love is strong we can do it."

"Sometimes I wish I was you. You don't know what my life is like."

"You need a man in your life. What did you do last night?" Judy changed the subject.

"I watched Terms of Endearment." Sarah was good at lying to her sister. She had been doing it for four years. So far, Judy didn't have any idea that Sarah was a stripper and a prostitute. She had no clue.

"Beth. Please get your overnight bag. Aunt Sarah is ready to bring you to her house."

"Okay, Mommy." Beth got up and grabbed her bag. She went to her mom and hugged her. Then Beth put on her red wool coat. It was dressy. "Will you be okay without me, Mommy?"

"Sure, honey. Mommy is going out on a date tonight. I'll have my cell phone with me in case you need to call me."

"Yes. Go have a good time tonight. Are you ready, Beth?"

"Yes, Aunt Sarah." Beth followed Sarah to the van. Beth sat in the back seat and buckled her seat belt. Sarah got in

the front seat and put the keys in the ignition The started to drive away.

"I think we'll arrive at the movie theater pretty soon. Tangled is playing. She is supposed to be Rapunzel. It looks really cute. We'll get some popcorn and soda. I also have change for the arcade."

"My friend, Lucinda saw Tangled. She liked it."

The girls parked at the movie theater, bought their tickets and then bought their buttered popcorn and soda. Sarah also let Beth have a box of Junior Mints. They played a few games and then went in and picked out their seat. Sarah liked to sit at the back. Beth liked the middle.

In a few hours the movie was done. Sarah and Bath walked back to the car. Once at Sarah's house, the girls got out of the car. Beth walked to the front porch. Resting on the steps was a bouquet of black roses. Beth stared at them for a minute. "Aunt Sarah, who would send you black roses?"

"I don't know. We'll throw them out."

"It's kind of creepy. Nobody likes black roses. Red roses are pretty. I like the pink ones."

"Me too," Sarah said. Beth and Sarah walked inside the house. "I bought a container of cookie dough. Are you up for making cookies?"

"Sure."

They went into the kitchen. Beth watched as Sarah pulled out a pizza stone. She placed the tub of cookie dough on her granite counter. Both of them got spoons and started placing scoops on the stone. Then Beth got a scoop and started eating it raw. I love chocolate chip. These are going to be good cookies." Sarah tossed the black roses into her white trash can. There was no note with the roses this time. At least when she tossed them in the trash she didn't have to see them. It was as if the black roses didn't exist.

Fifteen minutes later the first batch of cookies were done. Sarah put another batch in the oven and placed the cookie dough container back in the refrigerator. They ate one of the hot cookies. Sarah liked them best when they came right out of the oven.

"Would you like to draw a picture?"

"Okay."

"My paper is in the end table. My markers are in a basket on top of the paper."

Beth liked to draw pictures. Judy was always putting them on the refrigerator.

"I think I'll draw a picture of a horse."

"Do you have art in school?"

"Yes. Lucinda sits next to me. Sometimes she copies my pictures. I told Miss Jensen and Lucinda got in trouble."

"She should make her own pictures. You do your own thing and its original."

About an hour later it was six pm. Sarah was in the kitchen making a pizza. Beth loved mushrooms on her pizza. Sarah decided for half mushroom and half pepperoni. She shoved it in the oven and set the timer for twenty minutes. A half hour later, they were in the kitchen table eating the pizza.

At seven pm, they began to watch the Iron Giant. Beth picked it out. Sarah made a batch of popcorn.

At seven thirty there was a knock on her door. Sarah stood up and went into her mudroom. She opened the door and was surprised to see Officer George Trent. She reluctantly let him in. "Didyou find any fingerprints on those notes?"

"No. Whoever sent the messages used gloves. I need to ask you some questions about Teddy Barrington."

"Teddy Barrington?" Sarah was surprised. Why would Officer Trent be asking her about him?

"Where were you last night?"

"I was at Tangoes. Why?"

"We found Teddy dead in room seven this morning. We've found your fingerprints at the crime scene. We need to bring you down to the station now for questioning."

"Now? I've got my niece with me tonight."

"You'll need to arrange for her to stay with someone."

Sarah got her phone and called Judy. She answered on the third ring.

"Judy. Something came up and I need to bring Beth back. Sorry."

"What is it?"

"It's personal."

"Okay. I'll be back at the house in fifteen minutes. I'll see you soon." Judy hung up the phone.,

George said, "Drop her off and then I'll expect to see you down at the station." George left Sarah's house. Sarah got Beth ready to go.

"How come I have to go home?"

"Something important came up. Sorry. Get your bag. We'll meet your mom at your house." She didn't want to tell Beth where she had to go.

Beth hopped into the van. She was disappointed as she had wanted to spend the rest of the night at Sarah's house. Sarah drove towards Judy's house. She was glad that she didn't have to get in the police car. She didn't want to have to explain that. What had happened to Teddy? She had left him alive. Who had murdered him? Why would someone want him dead?

Sarah wondered what was going to happen. She knew she hadn't murdered him. She hadn't liked him forcing

himself on her, but she didn't have it in her desire to murder him. She didn't want death on her hands.

Beth sat quietly on the way back. Sarah was lost in her thoughts.

"Mom said we might get a puppy."

"That would be nice. You'd have to take good care of it."

"I'd be a good puppy owner."

Sarah pulled into Judy's driveway. Beth climbed out and went into the house. Sarah followed her in.

Judy looked at Sarah. "What do you have to do?"

"I've got some things to take care of." She said vaguely.

"All right. Does it have to do with a man? Are you using protection?"

"I'm not dating anyone right now. I haven't met Mr. Right." Sarah said. "I've got to go. I'll call you later in the week."

"Aunt Sarah got black roses on her porch today."

"Really? Who sent them?" Judy looked surprised.

"I don't know who sent them. It's really creepy. I gave the notes to the police. They didn't find anything."

Sarah left and got in the van. She drove to the police station. Once there, George put Sarah in the interrogation room. Sarah waited for someone to come in. Officer Larry May came in and sat across from Sarah. "So, what did you do last night?"

"I came to Tangoes and got ready to dance. I'm a stripper."

"Benny says your also a prostitute. What led you to all that?" Officer May looked skeptical.

"I've got lots of money I have to pay back from my credit cards. I saw the ad it a paper four years ago for exotic dancers. I came down to Tangoes and immediately started

working for Benny. At first I was nervous, but soon got used to it. I'm good at what I do."

"You enjoy men filling up your g-string with money? I hear that they get to touch you. You know that is illegal. Benny is getting away with a lot." Said Larry.

"Aren't we here to talk about Teddy?"

"Okay. When did you first see Teddy?"

"He was seated near the stage. I gave him a lap dance and he gave me some good tips."

"Is that all?"

"He paid for my services after the bar closed. He paid me five hundred dollars for him to fuck me. I liked it. I'm a horny girl." Her lips curved up into a wicked smile.

"Did you wear red licorice underwear?" He grinned at Sarah.

"Why?"

"Answer the question, Sarah. You're in deep crap. Right now we've got you all over the crime scene."

"Yes. I wore red licorice underwear. Did you eat the evidence? Would you like me to wear some for you?" She smiled demurely.

"Are you asking me to pay for your services? Are you into whips and chains too?" Larry grinned at the thought of that.

"Teddy wasn't into that. He liked my pussy. He bit my tits. Would you like to see the marks?" She stepped closer to Larry and pulled down her outfit and let her breast fall out of her bra. "Get a good look, you horny bastard."

"Funny. Don't expect to undress here." Larry smirked. "What did you do after he paid you the money?" He certainly got his eye full.

"After he paid me, I got dressed. Then he forced himself on me. He wanted more time with me. I fought him off me and got out. I left at two am. He was still alive when I

left. I didn't kill him. Seriously. I'm not a killer. Someone must have come in after I left. I got to my car and found some black roses on my car. I have a creep bothering me. Some of the messages are threatening. The person wants to see my blood on a knife. I didn't kill Teddy. I don't know who did. What about Benny? He was there when I left. I had to fork over two hundred dollars to him. He was there after I left."

"He was in his office until two ten am. His radio was on and he didn't hear anything. Did you see anyone on the way to your car?"

"No. I was alone. As far as I know. I could have been followed and not have known it. Can I go now?"

"Do you own a gun?"

"No." Sarah lied. "I have no weapons at my house. I don't know how to shoot a gun. Is that how he was killed?"

"Yes. Someone shot him in the forehead and stripped him of his clothing. Do you know his wife?"

"No. I didn't know Teddy before last night. He never discussed his private life. He just wanted to fuck me. Would you like to fuck me?" She got so close to Larry that he resisted the urge to back away. Something about Sarah turned him on.

"I'd probably get killed if I fuck you." Larry grinned and started laughing. "You can go now, but don't plan on leaving the state. We've got your fingerprints everywhere."

Sarah got up and walked closer to Larry. She pressed her body to him. He pushed her away. Sarah left the station. Larry looked at her ass on the way out. He was a pig. Sarah figured that someone came in after her and shot him. How dare Officer May be suspicious of her. She didn't do anything wrong.

George arrived in South Haven around eight pm. He knocked on the red door of a large house in an expensive neighborhood. A woman with black hair answered. She was wearing an apron over a pink turtleneck and tan dress pants. She had cobalt blue eyes and in her ears were pretty green earrings. "Mrs. Barrington?"

"Yes?"

"I'm Officer George Trent. It's about your husband, Teddy. When did you see him last?"

"In the afternoon. He came home for lunch and packed his luggage. He's away in Washington for the weekend. Why? Is he in trouble?" Her face suddenly looked serious. She gently pushed a strand of hair behind her ear. Her earrings shined in the light.

"I'm sorry to be the one to tell you, but your husband has been murdered."

She put her hands to her face and cried. "No. It can't be. You must have him confused with someone else!" She began to weep and the rims of her eyes turned red.

"No. We've identified him as Teddy Barrington. The owner of Tangoes told us his name. He knew about you and your boys."

"Jason is ten and Lorin is nineteen. I didn't know that he went there."

"Tangoes is a strip club. Your husband paid five hundred dollars for a prostitute last night. He was found dead in a bedroom upstairs from the club. Someone shot him in the forehead. They stripped him of his clothing. Do you know who would want him dead? Did he have any enemies? Where did he work?"

"He worked for Earnst, Langston and Everet. It's a law firm in South Haven. Sometimes he had to travel. I can't think of anyone who would want to murder him."

"Who are some of his co workers?"

"Larry Salander was his boss. He has a family in Kingston. That's the next town over. They've been good friends for years. Russell Jones is another lawyer. He's single and lives in South Haven. He's been with the company for five years. There's Betty Sims. She's another lawyer with the company. She's younger and has a family in Kingston. I think she has two little girls. Her husband works for a construction company. I can't imagine any of them killing him."

"It seems as if your husband has led a double life. Maybe he never traveled. How has your relationship been?"

"Normal. We've had a very good relationship. Sex at least a few times a week. I'm extremely shocked that he went to a hooker. I can't ever imagine him doing that. Did she kill him?"

"I'm not sure. She's been questioned by my partner. I haven't spoken to him yet. We did find her fingerprints all over the scene." Mrs.Barrington looked mortified. She was a little nervous too. George found out that most people he talked to were usually nervous or jittery around cops. It camewith the territory.

"Can I see my husband?"

"Do you want to? It's not a pretty sight. You might want to arrange for a closed coffin."

"When can I arrange for a funeral?"

"He's being autopsied today. Possibly over the next few days. Do you know a Sarah Fisher?"

"No. I can't say that I have. Is she the hooker?"

"Yes. She left him a two am last night. Anywhere from two am to two ten am he was killed. I plan to find his killer, Mrs. Barrington."

"He leaves behind two sons. They're going to be heartbroken. I still can't believe that he's gone. I think I need to see his body to be sure."

"Thank-you again for your time. I'm truly sorry that I had to be the one to tell you. It's never easy on the family. " Officer Trent left her house and drove back to the station. Earlier he had called Susan to tell her he would be late. He was going to stop by her house later in the evening. Once inside the station he talked to Larry. "So what did Sarah have to say? What do we know about her?"

"She's a prostitute. She's expensive. She gets five hundred bucks an hour but has to pay Benny two hundred after she's done. She came onto me."

"Holy crap. Did she confess to killing him?" George looked at Larry. Larry was single and he was a lady's man. There had been lots of women but Larry wasn't ready to settle down.

"No. She said she fucked him for an hour and then supposedly she left him alive at two am. She said she got to her car and found a black rose on the windshield. So her creep was in the area. What if she's just concocting a story about someone sending her roses? What if she's just making it up. Maybe she is putting the roses on her victim. She could be lying to us. I don't really believe her." Larry wanted to nail her. Yet she enticed him.

"Maybe it's connected to the killer. The black roses is the killer's signature. Creepy."

"Have you found out anything?"

"I went to pay a visit to Mrs. Barrington. She has two boys. That means two boys without a father. I'll go visit the law office where he worked tomorrow. I think they're open on Saturday. If not I'll find out where some of his co workers live and pay them a visit. I'm heading over to stay with Susan now. I'll see you tomorrow."

George got in his car and drove to Susan's house. Once there, he knocked on her door. She opened the door. "Sorry I'm late. I bought you a box of chocolates. They're dark chocolate."

"Thank-you. Come on in. Would you like some coffee and blueberry pie? I baked earlier this evening."

"Okay." George walked in and sat down in her kitchen. She had white kitchen chairs. Her kitchen was painted an olive green with white trim. Susan opened her cupboard and pulled out a New England Patriots mug and poured some coffee. She put in two creams and three sugars. Sheknew how George liked his coffee. "Anything new in the investigation?" Susan asked.

"I talked to Teddy's wife. She didn't know anything. She told me about his co workers. I'll talk to them tomorrow." George drank his hot coffee. Sometimes George didn't always finish his coffee, so he kept microwaving it. "This is really good pie. You're a good cook."

"Just wait until you try my chocolate pie. It's really good. Maybe I'll make it next week. My mother bought me a bunch of cookbooks."

"How did the evidence turn out?"

"Definitely Sarah. I found her fingerprints all over Teddy. I pulled the bullet out of Teddy. I went to the funeral home earlier today. The killer shot him with a 9mm gun. I extracted a .22 caliber bullet. There's no bruises on his body. It was a clean kill except for the blood. No fingerprints besides Sarah. "

George and Susan moved into the living room. She had a fire burning in the brick fireplace. The room was painted purple. Susan had several reproduction paintings done by Marc Chagall hanging on the wall. She had a corner curio cabinet that was filled with pretty china plates. She had some figurines of dogs on the mantle of the fireplace. She

had a Siamese Tortie Point kitten named Sukie. The kitten was resting on a rug near the fire.

George and Susan were sitting on the couch. Suddenly George put his hands on Susan's waist. His lips grazed hers with passion. Susan wrapped her arms around George's neck. Quickly he began to unbutton her shirt. Underneath she wore a white bra. His hands fumbled with her straps. Her bra fell loosely around her breasts. George pulled at it and tossed her bra onto the floor. His lips grazed hers with a passion that smoldered into burning flames. Then his lips found her shoulders and then her nice round breasts. George began to caress her breasts. Susan moaned and arched her back. She quickly undid his uniform and stripped down to his Hanes underwear. Her body tingled as he touched her. She wanted more of flaming passion.

Soon they found themselves on the carpeted floor making love. George kissed Susan with loads of energy. At first his kisses were soft and gentle. The kiss deepened into fierce desire. Susan massaged his hairy chest. Susan's nylon stockings were still on. George lifted one of her legs and thrust his dick into Susan's vagina. She was wet and hot for George. She rolled on top of him and pushed into his penis. George caressed her breasts tenderly. She screamed in delight.

Susan's black hair fell around her delicate face. George began kissing her breasts with complete tenderness. Susan had perky little tits. She lowered her body so he could suck on them.

The fire in the fireplace cast a glow upon Susan's body. George climaxed and then pulled out. He rested next to Susan. "That was much better than blueberry pie."

"You bet." Susan began kissing his chest as she rested her naked body next to his.

For a little while George forgot about the murder. He didn't want to think about dead naked bodies. He was baffled that they couldn't find the murder weapon. He was determined to solve the murder.

Sarah got back to her house. She had left the lights on. She got out of her car and locked the door. She stepped onto her porch. She stopped at the doorway. Her door was open ajar. It wasn't how she left it. Sarah stepped off her porch for a minute and checked around the yard. She saw no broken windows. She went back to the door. She hesitated. Slowly she stepped inside. She walked cautiously through her mudroom. It was empty. She went into the living room. The bowl of popcorn had been scattered onto the floor. The blue pillows on her couch had been slashed and the white stuffing was spilling out. A vase full of flowers had been knocked over and the flowers tumbled to the floor. Water spilled from the vase. A lion figurine had been smashed and the shards were everywhere. Black roses were visible in the middle of the floor.

A note was next to one of the roses. She picked it up and read it. It said Murderess. Whore. Die, bitch."

She dropped the note to the floor. She was really shocked that the person dared to enter her house. She felt very threatened. She ran into the kitchen and grabbed a sharp butcher knife. She wasn't sure if the intruder was still inside the house. She slowly walked up the stairs. She opened the door to her bedroom. Her rose pillows were also slashed and the stuffing was tossed on the floor. She saw another black rose resting on her bed. She grabbed her purple cell phone and called the police station. "This is Sarah Fisher. I live on 33 Leighton Lane in South Haven. I've had an intruder in my house. Could you send someone over to my house to investigate?"

"I'll send someone right over," said the receptionist. "Are you safe?"

"I think so. It looks like the person is gone. I don't see any sign of anyone."

"Be careful. Someone will be there soon." The receptionist

hung up the phone. Sarah looked at the ominous black rose on her bed. She screamed, "Why me?"

In ten minutes she heard a knock on her door. She ran to it and opened it. Officer Larry May was standing in the doorway. "What time did you come back? How could you tell someone was here?"

"It was about eight pm. The door was ajar. I came in to see my living room trashed and my pillows in my bedroom were slashed."

"What are you doing with that knife?"

"I was protecting myself." She forgot she was still holding it in her clenched hand. She placed it on her mudroom chair. Larry walked into the living room and looked at the damage. He saw the slashed pillows and the broken figurine. He saw the black roses on the floor. He picked up the note and looked at Sarah. She seemed to have fear in her eyes. Was it genuine fear or was she a really good actress? Larry was thinking that she planted the roses there herself. She didn't have a good alibi the night that Teddy was murdered. Her fingerprints were everywhere. Larry was getting the feeling that Sarah had staged the intruder, when indeed it was really Sarah that planned the whole thing. She had a motive to kill Teddy. He had attacked her. "Show me the bedroom." He had had enough of the scene in the living room. He was curious to see how erotic her bedroom was. What was a prostitute's bedroom like? He suddenly had his mind in the gutter.

"Would you like me to take it all off in the bedroom? You would really enjoy a good romp." Larry grinned. Then he followed her upstairs to the bedroom. He watched her walk in. He studied her ass. He thought of grabbing her and fucking her hard. She practically invited him to do so. He kept his thoughts to himself. He kind of wanted her

though. He wondered if he should just press her against a wall and see what happened. Probably not a good idea.

He examined the slashed pillows and the black rose. Was it her knife that had hacked at the pillows? He thought so. On a whim, he lifted the pink blankets. There it was staring him in the face. He then looked at the black rose. Did she sit down and paint them black? "Do you have black paints?"

"Yes. I do. Why?"

"I was just wondering. What kind of paints do you have?"

"They're acrylic. Why are you asking? You could get yourself naked and I could paint you black. I could give you a good blow job." He eyeballed her for a minute. Sheer delight was on his face.

Larry looked at the thing he discovered under the blanket. He pulled out a plastic bag from his pant pocket and bagged the evidence he found.

Sarah stared at the 9mm revolver. It shocked her to see it. It was hers, but she had kept it in her drawer. The intruder had placed it in her bed. "That's not mine," she lied.

"We'll see about that. This happens to be evidence now. I'll take the rose too. I'll need to see your paint. That's evidence too."

Larry followed her downstairs and into the kitchen. She opened a drawer and pulled out a rather large container of black acrylic paint. Larry leaned in closer to Sarah and stuck his hand in her pants for a minute. "I'll have to take a rain check on that blow job." He pulled his hand out and walked out the front door. She wondered why he needed her paints. That was beyond her imagination. He didn't once ask if she needed protection. That would have been nice. She locked her door behind him. Sarah watched as the police car drove away. She felt unsafe and she didn't quite trust Officer May.

Yet she liked tempting him. He would break down sooner or later. She looked outside past her yard. A woman was out walking her dog.

There was an idea. Maybe she should get a dog. A nice dog would give her added protection. She always liked pug dogs, but maybe she needed something larger like a golden retriever. She thought of places to look for a dog. There was the shelter. Maybe she could find someone who breeds dogs. It was getting late. Suddenly she heard a noise from her cellar. She went to the kitchen. The white cellar door was near there. She went to the door and stood there a moment. She listened for a sound but she was only greeted by silence. It was profound. She didn't want to hear another creepy noise. She locked the door. She wasn't a fan of dark musty cellars. The silence wasn't calming. It was as if she were waiting her worst horror. Was she beginning to live in a real nightmare?

She went back to the living room and sat on the couch. She grabbed her poetry journal and tried to write some verses. Sometimes writing relieved her. She wrote until ten pm. She set down the book and went to the kitchen. She opened her refrigerator and poured herself a glass of lemonade. After drinking it she went upstairs and put on her black lingerie. She retired to her soft bed.

She woke up the next morning at eight thirty. She stood up and went to the window. It was raining outside. It was pouring hard. She looked at her mailbox. She feared the thought of seeing another black rose later.

Black death. Was it foreseeable in her future? She didn't want to die. She wanted to be freeof her tormentor.

She called a dog breeder. There was a woman in Kingston who had some golden retriever puppies for sale. Her name was Betty. Sarah set up an appointment to visit the puppies on Monday.

She looked at herself in the mirror. Everything about Sarah was provocative. She loved black lingerie. Sarah got dressed. She put on a white bra and a skimpy white thong. Then she pulled on a low cut pink shirt and a pair of blue jeans. She decided to clean up the mess in the living room. She grabbed her white dustpan from the kitchen and went into the living room. She got down on her hands and knees and began to sweep away the broken lion. She threw the black roses in the trash. She put the note in the drawer of her end table.

After she was done, she left the house, got in her car and drove to the local pet store. She would slowly prepare for a puppy.

Friday at eight am Officer May arrived at the station with a large cup of coffee and a bag of donuts. He was hungry. The night before he had dropped off the gun, the rose and the jar of paint with Susan. Susan was in the lab working on the evidence. She had told Larry that she would be done at nine am.

Larry sat in the office and ate his donuts. He got Bavarian cream. It was his favorite. He loved the custard filling. Immediately he thought of Sarah's cream. Would it taste like custard? He drank his coffee and studied his notes on the murder. He looked at all the pictures he had taken of the crime scene. The autopsy had been done and Teddy had most likely died instantly. From a bullet to his forehead. It had been lodged in his brain. Susan had extracted the bullet and put it in a baggie.Teddy had been shot by a 9mm gun.

Larry thought back to putting his hand in Sarah's pants. The blow job sounded good. He remembered that she had been quite wet. Hot. Larry stood up and went into the bathroom that was down the hallway. He jerked off while thinking of Sarah.

At nine am Larry walked to the lab to see Susan. Susan was wearing a peach cashmere sweater and a brown skirt underneath her lab coat. Her hair was up today.

"Hello, Larry. So you're ready to find out the results?"

"What do you have for me?"

"The gun is the same one used on Teddy. The fingerprints on the gun are Sarah's. It's a perfect match. She may be guilty. The paint from the jar is the same paint on the rose. They're both acrylic. I'd say that you have enough to arrest her."

"Sounds good. I've been wanting to nail her. Thanks, Susan. Where's George?"

"I think he was headed over to Teddy's place of work. He said he has several places to go to today."

"I think I have enough evidence for a warrant to search Sarah's house. I'll see you later, Susan."

"Bye."

Officer Trent arrived at the law office at nine thirty. Immediately he was buzzed up to the fourth floor. He was led into a bright room. There were a lot of black leather chairs. George sat in one. There was a man with white hair sitting across from him. He was wearing a red oxford shirt and a striped tie. He was dressed in tan dress slacks. He was of a medium build. "Hi, my name is Larry Salander. What can I do for you, Officer Trent?"

"I'd like to ask you some questions about Teddy Barrington."

"It's awful. I can't believe he was murdered. I saw it on the news yesterday."

"Where were you on Thursday evening?"

"I was at home with my family. I got home at six and went to bed at nine thirty."

"Have you ever been to Tangoes?"

"I've heard of it, but I can't say that I've been. It's a strip club, right? I can't believe that Teddy went there. I thought he had a good marriage. He was a good lawyer. He got along with everyone. He had a good sense of humor. He was always telling jokes."

"Can you think of anyone who wanted him dead?"

"Not really. It baffles me that someone would want to kill him. Do you think that it could be a serial killer?"

"We're looking into things. So far we have leads on a prostitute named Sarah Fisher. Ever heard of her? She's also a stripper at the club."

"I honestly don't know any strippers. My wife would have my head on a platter if I ever set foot in a strip club. Anything else I can help you with?"

"No. I guess that's it. Thank-you for your time."

"No problem." Larry watched George leave the room.

George next went into another room. The walls were peach and there were several green chairs. He saw Russell Jones seated behind a desk. It was cluttered with books and lots of papers. Russell had long, black hair. It was tied back in a ponytail. He wore a striped oxford shirt and blue jeans. He was tall and thin. He had a square jaw.

"Hi, Russell. I'm Officer George Trent. I'd like to ask you about Teddy. Do you have a minute?"

"I'm rather busy with phone calls but I can spare a few minutes. What would you like to know?" Russell looked perplexed.

"First of all, where were you on Thursday evening?"

"I went to the Thirsty Turtle with a few of my friends. We had some food and drinks. I went home around eleven and went to bed. I played my guitar for a little bit before I settled down. It's a hobby of mine."

"Do you ever play in a band?"

"I did a few years ago. We were named Black Sheep. Now I just play for fun."

"Were you good friends with Teddy?"

"We went out for a few beers once in a while. We were friends. I hear that the funeral is tomorrow. Are you going?"

"I'm not sure what I have planned."

"His wife is devastated. His boys are now fatherless."

"Were you friends with his wife?"

"June is a good woman and a good mother. I admire her. They've had me over for supperonce in a while. She's a good cook. Teddy loved his wife. I'm surprised that he was with a hooker."

"Sarah Fisher. Do you know her?"

"No. I've never been to Tangoes."

"I never said that's where she worked. You've heard of Tangoes?"

"I know it's a strip club. One of my friend's went there once."

"What is his name?"

"Bernie Blackmore."

"Did he ever visit the girls after the show?"

"Not that I know of. Is it important?"

"We're looking at anything. Any information would be great."

"That's about all I know, Officer."

"Okay. Thanks. I'll let you get back to your phone calls. Sorry to bother you."

"Anything to help the investigation."

Last George found Betty Sims in another room. The walls were white and there was a lovely painting of a landscape on one wall. There were several diplomas on the wall. Betty was leaning overlooking at some of her files. She was five foot eight inches. She wore an Armani dress suit and high heels that were black. She had curly brown hair and blue eyes. Her hair was pulled back into a ponytail.

"Hello, officer. May I help you?"

"Betty Sims?"

"That's me." She was gorgeous. If George wasn't dating Susan, Betty would be his type.

"What do you know about Teddy?"

"He was a nice guy. He was funny, good looking and thoughtful. He was good at his job."

"Where were you on Thursday night?"

"I was home putting my girls to bed. Sally and Jean go to bed around eight o'clock. I had finished putting them to bed and then I watched Gray's Anatomy. I like that Patrick Dempsey. He is hot and sexy."

"My girlfriend likes that show too. Was Teddy a good friend?"

"He was nice, like I said. However, one day a few months ago he came into my office and tried to kiss me. I pushed him away and told him I was a married woman. Maybe he was unhappy in his marriage. It didn't really show until that moment. It made our friendship a little awkward."

"Did he ever tell you about going to Tangoes?"

"No. He never did. Although on Wednesday I went into his office and found a phone number on his desk. It said Sarah. I just thought it was one of his clients."

"That would be a stripper. Her name was Sarah Fisher. What did you do with the phone number?"

"I called her number. I didn't leave a message."

"Have you ever seen her?"

"No."

"Do you know of anyone who would want to kill Teddy?"

"Not really. He said someone was prank calling him a few years ago, but it can't be related."

"Well, you never know. Can you give me your number in case I have more questions for you?"

"Sure." Betty reached for a pink sticky note and jotted down her number. "Here it is. I'm usually home after six. I've got small girls so home is usually where I am."

"Are you a good mom?"

"You bet I am."

"That's good. Thank-you for your time. I'll let you get back to what you were doing."

"You're welcome." Betty glanced back at her files.

George left the building. He got in his car and went back to the station. First he went to see Susan. He needed a romantic break. "Hi, honey. You look pretty today."

"Thank-you. That deserves a kiss." George kissed her gently on the lips. She wrapped her arms around him. "Have you had lunch yet?"

"No. I have a body to autopsy in a half hour. So I'm headed to the funeral home soon. There was a suicide in Kingston last night. A teenage girl was found dead in her bedroom. Drug overdose. I'm going to do the autopsy to confirm it. The parents said she left a note. They usually do."

"How about when you're done we'll go to Moe's for some lunch. They always serve those nachos with their food."

"Okay. It'll take me an hour and a half to do the autopsy. Oh by the way, Larry found a gun in Sarah Fisher's bedroom. Her fingerprints are all over it. It's a 9mm like the gun that killed Teddy. Larry thinks she's lying. She probably killed him. She happened to be the last person that saw him. It fits. Larry thinks she's staging the black roses and the threat notes. She's a good pretender."

"I'll go talk to Larry." George kissed her again and then left the room.

He found Larry in the office eating a slice of pizza.

"Susan told me the news about Sarah. Are you going to arrest her?"

"Yes. I can't seem to get a hold of her. She's not answering her phone."

"Well, you know where to find her tonight."

"You bet."

George went back to his office and wrote down some notes about the lawyers. Betty Sims had some good information. Then he called the receptionist at the station. "Hello, Lucy. Can you look up a Bernie Blackmore? I need to know a phone number and an address."

"Sure. I'll call you back soon."

"Thank-you, Lucy."

Ten minutes later Lucy called him back and gave him a phone number. Bernie lived in South Haven. He thanked her and hung up.

After a nice lunch with Susan, George sat in his car and drove out to South Haven. He stopped near an apartment building. He went to the second floor and knocked on apartment number three. A bulky man with red hair appeared in the doorway. He looked like he hadn't shaved in three days. He looked like he worked out at a gym. "I did nothing wrong, officer."

"Bernie Blackmore?"

"That's me. What's wrong, officer?"

"Do you know Russell Jones?"

"Yes. He's a friend of mine. I haven't seen him in a while."

"Are you going to let me in?"

"Sorry. Come in. The place is a mess."

"Where were you on Thursday night?"

"I was having some beers at Tangoes. Why?"

"Do you know Sarah Fisher?"

"She was a dancer. She had nice tits and a good behind, man. Boy could she move. Good singer too."

"Do you watch her often?"

"I've watched her a few times."

"Have you ever seen her after the show?"

"No. I did give her some tips. She let me fondle her g-string and she gave me lap dances. I never saw boobs shake quite like that. I tell you it's a primal thing."

"What's that?"

"Men looking at women. Seeing tits are a real turn on. Sarah was hot!"

"I left at eleven thirty. I sure wish she'd give me a blow job."

"Do you know Teddy Barrington?"

"No. Never heard of him." He picked a piece of bacon off his plate and ate it.

"Do you own a gun?"

"No. I've never touched a gun."

"Do you have access to black paint?"

"No. I'm not an artist. I'm a mechanic. I don't have any paint in my house."

"Do you buy roses?"

"No. I haven't bought roses for two years. It's been two months since I broke up with my girlfriend."

"What was her name?"

"Ava Peabody. She was pretty. We kept fighting so I broke it off. She chased me for a month. She kept hounding me to go out with her again. Finally she stopped."

"Do you like porn sites, Bernie?"

"I do. I've got some favorite websites. I've got a stack of Hustler magazines in my bedroom. Good jerking off."

"Do you know where Sarah Fisher lives?"

"No, man. I don't know much about her. All I know is that she's a good stripper. Is that it for the questions? I've got to get ready for work."

"That's it for now, thanks."

Bernie slammed the door on George. George was stunned. He wasn't expecting that. Bernie had an alibi. But he knew Sarah Fisher. That was something.

George went to the neighborhood park to kill some time. He got out of the car and sat on the bench. He watched some of the children playing on the playground equipment. George wanted to start a family. He wanted Susan's children.

That evening Sarah drove to her house to change her clothing. She walked upstairs to her bedroom and looked through her lingerie. She picked out a skimpy black thong. She chose not to wear a bra. She slipped on black thigh highs and a pair of black stilettos with rhinestones on them. She then slipped on a tight fitting red dress. She grabbed her cherry red lipstick and smeared some on her lips. She added thick eyeliner to her eyes. She put her hair up into a ponytail.

At nine thirty, she drove to Tangoes. She walked straight into the dressing room. She was thankful that there were no black roses this evening. She hated those things. Ten minutes later, Benny waltzed in. He quickly pushed Sarah to the floor. His thick hands pushed up her dress and pulled down her thong. He undid his knaki pants and pulled out his penis. He violently thrust himself into her vagina. He banged her hard against the cold floor. He hit her repeatedly. His hands grasped her breasts and squeezed them. He pulled out. "Suck my dick, Sarah. Now."

Sarah slowly got up and grabbed hold of his massive penis. He was very hard. She sucked on it and let him push it deeper into her mouth. He groaned and had an erection. She sucked him fiercely. After twenty minutes he pulled out and stood up. He zipped his pants. Then he slapped her face. "Don't play games with me, Sarah. What did you do to Teddy? I don't want bad business here."

"I didn't kill him. You're raping me. That's bad business."

"Hey, the evidence points to you, bitch. You squeal on me, I'll send my thugs to beat you up."

Benny slapped her a few more times. "You're on in ten minutes." He tossed her to the floor as if she were a floppy rag doll. He left the room. Sarah felt like crying. She didn't

like him raping her, but she didn't want to feel the wrath of his thugs. Benny had power.

Ten minutes later Sarah stepped onto the stage. She began to dance erotically. She decided not to sing tonight. She had a sore throat. Tonight there were two dancers on the stage. Susie was also dancing. After a few minutes, Sarah and Susie took off their dresses. Suddenly they had nothing on except for panties. Susie had on a skimpy red thong. Susie shimmied and shook her big breasts. Both began to dance and slide . Sarah wrapped her legs around the pole. Susie slid to the bottom and did a split. Sarah arched her back and lowered her body to Susie. Susie had brown hair. Sarah slid her hands through Susie's hair. Susie's hand came up and caressed Sarah's body. Sarah stood up and started dancing closer to the edge of the stage. Then she slid to the edge and stepped into the audience. Suddenly to her left, she glimpsed the presence of Officer May. He was sitting in a chair drinking a beer. Sarah started giving him a lap dance. Suddenly she straddled him. Officer May caressed her breasts and then pushed her away. Sarah then danced near Susie. Both girls got men putting money in their g-strings.

Suddenly Sarah and Susie started fighting about a nearby guy who was putting money in Susie's g-string. Sarah was jealous and both girls started to attack each other. After a few minutes they stopped fighting and kissed each other on the lips for a minute. Susie wrapped her arms around Sarah's waist. Some of the men whistled. Then Sarah sat on a nearby man's lap and let him fondle her breasts.

Later, Sarah went back into the dressing room. Benny came in. "There's a man in room six that wants your services. Go see him now" It was one am. Sarah walked upstairs. She was wearing her dress again. There was a man with dark hair. He had blue eyes. He was wearing a red oxford shirt and a paisley tie. He wore blue jeans. He was very muscular.

Susie was sitting next to him. She was wearing a green wrap around dress. Her lips were painted ruby red.

"Sarah come here. Come sit on my lap. Please take off your dress." Sarah wriggled out of her dress and it landed on the floor. The man came closer and pulled at her thong. She let it slideto the floor by the dress. Susie took off her dress. She was wearing green thigh highs. She kept them on. Sarah kept on her black thigh highs. Sarah rubbed her body against the man's hairy chest. Susiebumped her cunt against his back. Sarah's hands undressed the man. Suddenly all three of them were naked. Sarah pressed her body against his while Susie groped him from behind. The man thrust his dick into Sarah's vagina. He fucked her hard. Susie penetrated him from behind.

Sarah sucked his cock and he felt himself come inside her mouth. Then Susie pressed her body against Sarah's. Susie caressed Sarah's breasts for ten minutes. Then Susie's tongue licked Sarah's big nipples. The man watched while Sarah and Susie bumped cunts. Susie's lips sucked hard on Sarah's tits. Susie's hands grabbed Sarah's lower waist and the two women began to kiss passionately. Susie fondled Sarah's ass. Sarah gently kissed Susie's tits.

The man pressed his body against Susie. She turned around and let him push his penis into her vagina. Sarah fucked him from behind. Both women wrapped their legs around him. They caressed him and each other. "Fuck me hard, girls. You horny women." Sarah got in front of him and let him eat her cream. She cried out and moaned as he tongued her clitoris.

Suddenly the door was busted open and Officer May stood in the doorway. He saw the man was busy licking Sarah's pussy.

He walked over to Sarah. He pushed her naked body against the red wall and hand cuffed her. He pressed hard

and fast. Larry was rough. Sarah pushed and shoved him. She put up a struggle. "You pig! You don't have any right to lock me up. No fucking way!" She tried to spit at him, but he pressed her face against the wall. She didn't like it. The small of her back was hurting and her wrists were bound tightly. She didn't like her naked body pushed against the wall. She also didn't like it that he had barged in on them. They were having too much fun.

"Sarah Fisher. You're under arrest for the murder of Teddy Barrington." Larry pushed her against the wall again and leaned against her so she couldn't move. His hand groped her vagina and he pushed his finger into her. "Too bad this had to end, huh." He grinned and pulled out his wet finger.

"You dick! I didn't kill him. Let me go!" She tried to move her wrists but it was no use. Susie and the man began to get dressed. Evidently time was up. Susie stared at Sarah. She was bewildered.

"Let me get dressed and collect my money!"

Larry thought about it. He rather liked it this way. He was in power over her. Finally he reluctantly uncuffed her and watched her get into her red dress and thong. Once she was dressed he handcuffed her and shoved her out the door. Sarah was pulled down the stairs and past the bar. Benny was sitting on a stool. "Where are you taking my girl? I need my money."

"She's being arrested." Larry handed Benny the two hundred dollars. They left the bar. Once outside the bar Sarah saw the squad car. It was still raining. There were puddles everywhere. Rain soaked Sarah's dress. Larry opened the back door and shoved Sarah inside. She landed on the hard blue seat. Sarah watched the raindrops trickle down the windows.

Larry drove her to the police station. Once he parked

in the lot, he got Sarah out of the car and pulled her inside the station. He brought her to a small jail cell and he shoved her inside and locked the door. The walls were made of gray stone and the metal bars were cold to the touch. Sarah felt humiliated and wrongly accused. "Why do you have reason to arrest me?"

"Your fingerprints were all over the gun. Explain that."

"It's not mine!" she lied.

"How come your fingerprints were on it?"

"Okay. It's mine. I didn't kill him. You've got to believe me. Someone broke into my house and used my gun. I kept it somewhere else in my bedroom. I didn't put it in my bed."

"You used it, you lying bitch. Admit it. You wanted to kill him and you got your chance. You don't have a good alibi." Larry grinned. He knew he had her locked up where she belonged. She looked really good behind bars. Maybe later he would come in and fuck her. Hard. He could get away with it. After all he was a cop. Cops could do anything that they wanted. They were the law.

"I didn't kill him. I swear I didn't kill him." Larry gave her the finger and left the room. He didn't want to listen to her. As far as he was concerned she was guilty as a black sheep. He knew it was her gun all along. What a filthy liar. At least now she was behind bars.

Sarah sat on a small bench. There was a green army blanket next to her. She rested her head in her hands. She began to cry. Warm tears slowly slid down her cheeks. She wiped away her tears with the back of her hand. How had she gotten into this mess? Why couldn't she have been like Judy? She was the good sister. She got married and had a daughter. She had a normal job. She wasn't sexually crazed like Sarah. Sarah had always been a wild child. Sarah smoked cigarettes when she was a teenager. She drank lots of alcohol when she turned twenty one. Sarah drank two or three bottles of white zinfandel a week. Some mornings she made herself a fuzzy navel as part of breakfast. Judy knew about the drinking and told her she should quit and go to therapy classes.

Judy never got into trouble. She married her high school sweetheart. The only messy thing in Judy's life was her divorce. But at least she lived a normal life.

Then Sarah met Benny and trouble found her. But the money was good. She owed a lot of money. Some nights she met with two johns and made one thousand dollars. After Benny took four hundred of it she was left with six hundred for one night's work.

Sarah tried to remember anyone that would stand out as threatening. She couldn't think of anyone. Deep down she knew she wasn't a murderess. Someone had set her up. Whoever broke into her house found her gun and planted it on her. That was the real killer. Sarah was angry with Larry. He had locked her up for the wrong reasons. She shouldn't be here. She should be driving home to her house right about now. It just wasn't fucking fair. No way. She hadn't laid a hand on Teddy. At least not violently. She hadn't used her gun in years. She tried target practice a few times after she got the gun. But the targets were Dr. Pepper soda cans. Inanimate objects. Absolutely harmless.

She thought again about stripping and prostitution. She liked the money. She was also used to the lifestyle. She liked selling her body. She had a good body. Why let it go to waste? Men liked her. She thought about fucking Officer May. He would be a good fuck. She also felt like hitting him. She was contradicting herself. At the same time she loathed him for locking her up. It was just thoughts. She really didn't plan on fucking him. He was a pig. Jesus. Come on. She had to figure a way to get herself out of this mess. She needed to convince them to let her go. They were chasing the wrong string up their ass. While she was behind bars a killer was out there possibly ready to strike again. Definitely not a good thing. Maybe she could talk to the other cop. That Trent guy. Maybe he could find it in his heart to see that she wasn't a cold blooded killer. She didn't have it in her. She cried some more until her eyes were red. Her mascara was running and she had black streaks across her face. She felt like a mess. Her thong was riding up her crotch and she felt uncomfortable. She didn't want to spend the night in jail. She didn't belong here. She screamed bloody murder. Maybe Officer May would come back in and she could beat him up and escape. Then she would be on the run. Maybe she could run to a new state, change her identity and start a new life. Could she really do that? It wasn't like her to just start fresh. maybe she could do it. Anyone could do it if they set their mind to it. Could Sarah turn into a good girl?

The man who had just fucked Sarah that night was driving home to Kingston. It was dark and the rain was drizzling down his windshield. He lit a cigarette and puffed a smoke. He thought of Sarah and Susie. He loved having sex with two women at once. It was awesome. It was every man's wild wet dream. He also found it titillating to watch them fondling each other. It was erotic. That damn cop had to interrupt them. It was upsetting. His hour with the girls hadn't been up yet. He still had to pay one thousand dollars for them. He had rather enjoyed licking Sarah's vagina. And those two girls kissing each other was something else.

He took a left turn and drove down a winding country road. Suddenly another car was behind him. The car drove really near him and started ramming into his car. The car drove fast and crashed into the side of his car.

The man stopped the car on the side of the road. He was upset that someone was wrecking his car. The other car parked in front of his car.

The man got out of the car and started walking towards the person in the other car. He stood in front of the car door. The person rolled down the window. The stranger stuck out a 9mm revolver and shot the man in the head. The person sent another bullet to his heart.

The man staggered for a few minutes and then fell to the ground. The person got out of the car and tossed a black rose onto the man. The man was stone dead at two am. The person put on gloves and stripped the man of his clothing. It was tossed in a garbage bag. The person drove away in a black Porsche.

The next morning at six am Larry arrived at Sarah's house with a warrant and her house keys. He opened the door and began his search. He started at the closed in porch. He found her leather bound notebook on the table next to the wicker chairs. He picked it up and flipped through it. It was mostly poetry. He read one page that read fuck Officer May. Really hard. Larry grinned. In her dreams. He didn't really plan on fucking her. Although he couldn't seem to get her off his mind. He was a dirty cop.

He set down the book next to a white blanket throw. There was a stray black petal from a black rose. Those black roses. He thought of her sitting in her wicker chair painting black roses. What a little devil. He had her where she belonged.

He went into the mudroom. There was a purple loveseat against the wall. There was lilac wallpaper on the wall. He saw a white chest of drawers. He opened the top drawer. There was a videotape. He grabbed it. There was a stack of photos. A bunch of them were Sarah's parents. underneath there was one of a man. On the back of the photo she had written Bernie. Larry grabbed the photo and put it in a baggie. It was probably evidence.

He went into the living room. He popped the tape into the video player and watched it. It showed Sarah taking her clothing off. Then it showed her having sex with a man. He looked like the man in the picture. The video tape showed Sarah sucking Bernie's dick. Her hands were rubbing his thighs and his testicles. Then Bernie fucked her hard. "You're my fucking black rose," the man said. Larry continued to watch them fuck. He felt like finding Sarah's bathroom to jerk off in. He pulled out the tape and set that and the picture on the coffee table. Under the coffee table was a pink photo album. He flipped through it. There were lots of pictures of Sarah with a young man. She looked younger in

the pictures. Larry figured it was an old boyfriend. Why did it end? Was Sarah terrible at relationships? Maybe she and Larry would be a good match. He thought about it. Could he get involved with a murderess? Come on.

He looked at Sarah's fireplace. It hadn't been used recently and there were old ashes caked in. Sarah had some old newspapers resting on the brick hearth. There was a white rug in front of the fireplace. Did she fuck men on it? He wondered. His mind was definitely in the gutter. He imagined himself lying naked on the rug. Then he imagined her sucking on his dick. What a thought.

Sarah had some Victorian figurines on the mantelpiece. There were a bunch of comfy pillows settled against a large picture window. Larry figured that she liked to rest there and maybe do her poetry. He really couldn't think of her as a writer. Sarah the prostitute was too much in his mind. The Sarah that lived in this house seemed different. She had expensive taste. Larry found one of her credit card statements in a drawer. No wonder she was a prostitute. Now it became a little more clear to him. She was a shopaholic. Wow. She must be a little too quick to spend her money.

There was a large oriental rug near her pink lazy boy chair. The floors were hardwood.

On her coffee table there was a vase filled with yellow roses. Where were the black roses? He wondered where she kept them. He opened a drawer to her end table. He found a pack of cigarettes and some matches. She was a smoker. He didn't think she was. He was discovering about her today. There was a purple tension ball. He pulled it out and squeezed it several times. He had a red one at home. There were a bunch of stray rubber bands and several unused .22 caliber bullets. He grabbed the bullets and put them in a baggie. Also in the drawer were some tweezers, pink craft scissors and a drawing. The picture was signed Beth.

Larry shut the drawer. Also on the coffee table was a book on Audrey Hepburn and several copies of Vogue. There was a piece of notepaper near her phone. It said ten am on Monday. He jotted it down in his black notepad. It could be of interest. Maybe she was going to kill someone else on Monday. Was Sarah a serial killer?

Against one wall was a hutch with glass cabinets. Inside there was a collection of chintz teacups and saucers. She had a pretty set of wine glasses. There were flowers etched on them. Her lower shelf had some mystery books by Iris Johannsen and Lisa Jackson. There was a porcelain doll resting next to some of the books. He thought back to one of those movies where an expensive piece of jewelry is hidden in a doll. You never know. Larry's mind was on a wild tangent. The doll had a really curly brown wig and was dressed in a pink taffeta dress. She had pantaloons on underneath and brown lace up shoes. She had a beautiful face. Maybe she let her niece play with the doll.

He walked into her kitchen and opened her cabinets. He mostly found food and dishes. She had plenty of china plates. There were more chintz teacups in the cabinet. How much money did she have on her credit cards? If she was married she couldn't do that.

There was a set of knives on the counter. She had an espresso machine and a coffee maker. A pink Kitchen Aid mixer was resting on her island. Her curtains in the kitchen were red gingham. She had a ceramic rooster on the top of a shelf. He opened it up and found two thousand dollars in it. It was her secret money jar. After finding nothing of real significance in her kitchen he walked up the beige carpeted stairs. He went into her bedroom. She had a pink floral comforter on her bed. Her sheets were white satin. Her curtains were pink and matched her pink walls. He imagined himself naked under her sheets. Then he imagined

himself dead. He felt a wave of horror wash over him. He couldn't have that happen. He walked over to her lingerie drawer and opened the top drawer. He found a pack of thirty edible underwear. He took one out and chewed on it. It tasted like strawberry. He ate it while he searched the room. The second drawer of her lingerie drawer contained lots of tassels. He picked one up. He thought of her massive tits. She had lots of g-strings. Most were black. She had a sexy black corset and lots of thigh highs.

In another drawer she had a whip and knitted handcuffs. Larry started laughing. He thought about that for a moment. Kind of kinky. Sarah was his kind of woman. Again he thought of fucking her hard. He picked up a lacy blindfold. Interesting. Maybe she could wear it. Better yet maybe he would wear it while she whipped him. He liked the thought of that. He could be into domination. It was his cup of tea. Fucking her hard was all that mattered.

He opened up her closet doors and found numerous pairs of stilettos. She owned lots of skimpy dresses. She also had a French maid's dress. She had a cop uniform for women. He was guessing those were for her stripping act. He found some sandalwood body lotion. He thought of massaging her breasts with it. He liked the smell of sandalwood. He found another drawer and opened it. There was a gun. He grabbed it as evidence.

He checked the drawer in her nightstand. It had some photos of men. One said Johnny. One said Burt. Another said Jeremy and the last one said Peter. He kept them all. Were they some of her johns?

He walked into her bathroom. He found nothing unusual in her medicine cabinet. Her shower curtain had orange fishes on it. Larry thought it was cute. She had a lace curtain on her window. She had pink rugs on the floor and a pink padded cushion was on her toilet. There was a

container of Tylenol on her counter. Maybe she suffered from headaches. He opened the container and swallowed a Tylenol. He had a massive headache.

He went back into the kitchen. He eyeballed the twenty bottles of white zinfandel. Maybe she had a drinking problem. He thought of himself. He was addicted to beer. He easily drank several cases of beer a week. He grabbed one of her honey buns from the counter and began to wolf it down. He was hungry.

He confiscated all the evidence and locked up her house. He had checked out her van before coming to the house. He had seen her Gucci purse and thought it was ridiculous. It had a leopard print on it. He headed back to the police station.

He parked the squad car outside and walked in. He went straight to the jail cell. Sarah was resting on the bench. He opened the door to her cell and walked in. "Who is Bernie, Johnny, Burt, Jeremy and Peter, bitch. Are you planning on killing them? I found your other gun. You know it's illegal to have guns. Do you have a permit for it?"

"Yes. I have a permit, asshole."

"Hey. Don't mouth off to a cop, you cunt." Larry stripped off his pants and showed her his penis. "Suck my dick, you filthy murderess. Do it now." Sarah got down on her knees and gave him a massive blow job. She felt like biting off his dick in the process. She decided not to be like Lorena Bobbit. When she was done he pushed her on the floor and locked her back up. He felt satisfied. He left the room and went into the break room for a cup of black coffee. There were more Bavarian chocolate donuts. He took one and went to the office to examine his evidence. He popped the tape of Sarah and Bernie into the VCR and watched it again. He had a big smile on his face. He loved her blow job. He wanted more. He knew where to find her. She was going to be in jail for a long time. He planned to have his way with her before she went to a larger prison. If he had his way she would be in jail for many years. He felt satisfied that he was putting her away. He felt that he had caught his killer. He had let a murderess suck his cock. For free. He didn't feel obligated to pay her anything. He wasn't sure if he should tell George about it. George might not like that. George was a good cop.

Later George came into the office and found Larry watching a video. "I've arrested Sarah. She's really guilty man. We found our killer."

"Are you sure it's her?"

"Her fingerprints are all over the gun. That's prime evidence. She has a serious motive. She admitted the gun was hers. I found another gun. It's the same gun that killed Teddy. What more do you want? I found pictures of some of her johns. Here's this raunchy tape."

"But she says she didn't kill him. Maybe she's not lying. Someone could have set her up. Come on Larry. Look at all the angles. She says she left him alive. Someone else could have done it. What about Benny? He was there after she left. Maybe he's the one who went up and shot him. We've got to look at everything. Maybe Benny was lying to us. He's a pimp. Maybe he had a motive to kill Teddy."

"No. It has to be Sarah. She's a rotten murderess. I'm not wrong on this." Larry looked peeved. He didn't like it that George might not be on his side. Larry was always right. He was never wrong. He remembered back to throwing Sarah against that wall. He had gotten his rocks off on that. He wished he could have seen the two girls wrapped around each other. He had seen them kissing on stage and wanted to see more of it. Maybe Sarah was a lesbian. That excited him. Maybe she killed because she didn't like men. It was a nasty thought that ran through Larry's mind. He was going to make sure she didn't get near a gun again. He didn't want her killing him. She'd have a motive for killing him now. Larry was bad. Larry didn't want George knowing about the drugs another dirty cop was giving him. So far George didn't know anything about it. Larry planned to keep it that way. Larry had quite the stash of marijuana in his house. He liked to get high. There was a thrill in it. He had tried cocaine before too. It was all off the clock.

He thought of her sucking on his cock again. Soon. He would go to her again later. It thrilled him. He wanted to come in her mouth again. Delicious.

George looked at the tape playing for a minute. Suddenly he recognized Bernie. "Hey, Larry. that's Bernie Sanderson. I interviewed him. This proves that he knew Sarah Fisher more than he told me. He said she only gave him a lap dance. Nothing more. This shows that she fucked him. Maybe he was one of her johns. He kind of lied to me. Maybe there is more to him than he was telling me. I wonder why he calls her my black rose. Maybe there is something to it. Larry, he could be a suspect. We should look into it. Maybe I should question him again. Pump him for more information. He could be in some deep shit for all we know. Remember, all angles. This may not be over."

Larry didn't like the sound of that. As far as he was concerned his number one suspect was now sitting in the jail cell. She was in a deep pile of shit. He wanted her locked up. He wanted his way, god damn it. Larry didn't like it that George was trying to change the fucking tune. This was his show. He wanted to bring her down. Really hard. And he wanted the blow jobs too. He wanted to shove his penis into her pussy. Larry was lost in thoughts of Sarah and didn't see the receptionist, Lucy Wilcox come into the room.

Lucy was short and had blond hair. It was thick and straight. She wore purple rimmed glasses over her brown eyes. Lucy was in her fifties. She wore a blue turtleneck underneath a matching pullover sweater. She wore a stylish skirt of moss green color. She wore a pair of brown Ugg boots. She was dressing for warmth.

George looked up and stopped watching the video. He had seen enough. "What's up, Lucy?"

"A woman called. She was out jogging on route 117 in

Kingston. She's discovered a dead man lying on the side of the road. She says it looks like he was murdered."

"We'll be right there." George turned off the video and looked at Larry.

"Hey, I was still watching that."

"You're done. Let's go. Maybe our killer is still at large."

Larry scowled and slowly got off his seat. He didn't want to go investigate a new murder. He wanted to finish the video and eat more donuts. Larry followed George out the door and they got into the squad car. George called the forensics team to let them know. They would be there soon.

Upon arrival, they immediately saw the woman jogger standing near the body.

"My name is Elizabeth. I was out jogging and stumbled onto his body. It was nine thirty when I found him. I haven't touched anything. This is my regular route. I live on Swedish Lane not too far from here."

"Are you okay? This is quite a morbid scene."

"I'm alright. Just a little shocked. It's not every day that one stumbles onto a dead body. I'm not sure how long he's been here."

"The coroner will decipher that one for us." Said George. Elizabeth had a long blond ponytail that was wrapped with a green band. She was tall and lanky. She wore a pink active wear top and form fitting black sweats. She wore Nike sneakers. She was pretty. Larry smiled at her and then started spreading yellow crime scene tape around the area. After Elizabeth answered some more questions they let her jog away.

They looked at the dead man. Larry recognized him. "That's the john that was with Sarah.There was another stripper with them."

There was a single black rose on the man's stomach. It looked like he was shot in the head and the heart. "That's brutal. We're looking at a cold-blooded killer. I don't think Sarah is your killer, Larry. She's in jail, so she couldn't have done this to him. Someone else is doing the killing. The black rose is the killer's signature. Maybe Sarah really is being threatened. It could all be connected. She could be in danger. We should give her some protection."

"You think she was set-up?" Larry felt disappointed. He was so sure it was Sarah. There goes his future blow jobs.

"Yes. Someone may have planted her gun in her bed. It explains why she keeps telling you she didn't do it. After seeing this, I think you need to let her go."

"Damn. I was so sure it was her."

"She's just guilty of being a prostitute, Larry."

"She may also be an alcoholic. She has a lot of alcohol in her kitchen. She's also a shopaholic. That explains the prostitution. She needs to sell her body to pay her bills."

"Let's go see if this guy has any identity. The killer must like to leave them naked." George walked over to the green Volkswagen that was parked near the body. He opened the door and checked in the glove compartment. He found the registration. The name on it was Johnston Billings.The address read 8 Cedar Lane in South Haven.

The forensics team arrived and began dusting the area for fingerprints, trace evidence and any sign of footprints. Larry pulled out a Polaroid camera and began taking photographs of the bullet wounds, the black rose and any other significant evidence that they could process. Later, George dropped him off at the station. The forensics team would later wrap the body in plastic and then a body bag. Johnston would be taken to the embalming room in the funeral home.

George drove out to Cedar Lane. He stepped out of the

car and walked over to the ranch style house. He kicked open the red door. He walked into a living room. The walls were painted white. There was a stack of Hustler magazines on the coffee table. There was a bong and a bag of marijuana near the magazines. There was a picture of Sarah and the other woman. Both were naked. George grabbed the picture and put it in his coat pocket. Johnston had a lot of DVDS. There was a whole set of the Friday the 13th movies. He also had the Shining and all the Halloween movies.

George found a bunch of check stubs in a drawer. Johnston worked for IBM. So he probably had a good paying job. He evidently had enough money to pay for two prostitutes. He saw no sign that Johnston was married. There was nothing feminine in the house. There were more slutty magazines underneath the end table. George thought of giving them to Larry. It was Larry's cup of tea. George remembered seeing Larry eyeballing a Hustler magazine one morning. He probably got his rocks off after that. George remembered looking at those magazines when he was a teenager. He had a favorite tree house he liked to hang out in. He and his friend, Jason would love looking at the women. George's mother finally found the magazines and threw them in the trash. George was heartbroken. George went on to date a few girls in high school. His first girlfriend was a girl that lived a few streets away. Her name was Carrie Matthews. He had liked her a lot. He took her to one of the high school proms.

George cast aside his old memories and walked into the kitchen. The kitchen walls were painted yellow and the curtains were green. He opened the refrigerator and found a case of Labatt's beer. He had English muffins, eggs and a loaf of bread. There wasn't much in his refrigerator. He opened the freezer and discovered stacks of hamburger patties, a bag of chicken tenders and potato puffs. There

were also some frozen chicken pot pies. Man food. On his kitchen counter was a day old bag of McDonald's food. It had been half eaten.

George checked out the bedroom. The walls were blue. Johnston had a waterbed. The comforter was black. On the floor there was a black bra. George grabbed it and bagged it. Johnston had some condoms on his nightstand. There was also a black alarm clock. Maybe Johnston had a girlfriend. There wasn't much else for evidence.

George left Johnston's house and drove to IBM. He parked the car and walked into the building. It was busy. There were large landscapes on the white walls.

George stopped in front of the receptionist. He pulled out his badge and showed it to her.

"What can I do for you, officer?" She had brown hair and cornflower blue eyes. She was in a yellow dress that had long sleeves. Around her neck was a pearl necklace. She looked at George with caution in her eyes.

"Johnston Billings. He worked for IBM. He's been murdered. What section did he work for?"

"Third floor. Ask for Iris Jacobs and Lesley Fry. They worked with him. They may be of help."

"Thank-you." George found the elevator, stepped in and got off on the third floor. George discovered Iris Jacobs at a booth in the middle of the room. "Iris Jacobs?"

"That's me." She was a small woman. She had dark black hair and brown eyes. She had thekind of hair that a man would want to tangle his hands into. She had a heart shaped face and a pale complexion. She was wearing a puffy red blouse and a stylish tweed skirt. She wore high heeled black dress pumps.

"Did you know Johnston Billings?"

"Yes. Why?"

"Where were you last night?"

"I went to the movies with a friend and then went home around eleven. What is the matter?"

"He's been murdered on route 117. He was shot in the head and the heart. He was last seen around one am to two am at Tangoes. What was he like?"

"He was quiet. He usually kept to himself. He was single but had a girlfriend named Julie. She works for Dunkin Donuts. That's a few streets away on Main St. She seems nice. I met her a few times."

"Can you think of any enemies he may have had?" He watched her reach for a stack of papers that were near her Dell computer. A picture of a little girl was in a pink frame on her desk. She had a cup of Dunkin Donuts coffee resting near the computer. He was keeping her from it.

"Not off hand. He seemed like an all around nice guy. He was a little rough around the edges."

"He paid for two hookers last night. Do you know anything about that?"

"No. I kept out of his private life. Wow. That's a man for you. Maybe he was a pervert. "

"Are you married?"

"Yes. I'm married to John Jacobs. He works for South Haven Hospital. He works in the ER. We have a little girl, Gracie. She's about three years old. She goes to a daycare. She got an earache earlier this week so I had to stay home with her on Tuesday."

"That's too bad. Sometimes they pick up more germs when they're in a daycare. My sister sends her kids to a daycare too. They're constantly getting sore throats or colds. Well, I won't take anymore of your time. Thank-you for your help. We're looking at all angles trying to find our killer." George walked away and next searched for Lesley Fry. He found her in a private cubicle near a large window. Lesley had red hair that was wound up in a bun. She had an oval face. She was wearing pink blush on her cheeks. She was clad in a revealing white blouse and a short black skirt. It barely covered her thighs. Her cleavage was supple. She wore white flats on her feet. She looked like the kind of girl that was quick to bed. He was guessing that she was easy.

"Hi, I'm Lesley." She nervously pulled at a strand of hair that was hanging near her gold hoop earrings. They shimmered in the daylight.

"I'd like to ask you some questions about Johnston Billings. Where were you last night?"

"I did a little shopping after work and got home to my place around nine thirty." She looked at George warily. "Did I do something wrong? I went to JCPenney s and TJMaxx. Those are my favorite stores. I love clothing."

"I can tell. You look great. My sister likes to shop too. I keep telling her that she is going to buy out Mikasa. Johnston was murdered anywhere from two am last night to nine thirty this morning. What was he like?"

"He flirted with me if that's what you want to know. I kind of liked it. I'm a single woman. I'm twenty six years old. Johnston was twenty eight. I'm playing the field. Yesterday he came in and told me he broke up with his girlfriend, Julie. He came onto me and said I had nice creamy breasts. He asked me if I wanted to have casual sex. I told him I wanted a little more in a relationship. I gave him my phone number. He didn't call me last night. When I got home, I watched Fried Green Tomatoes. But earlier that day we made out on my desk. We did have sex. I had a change of heart. It was great. I'm sad that he's gone. I was kind of hoping our relationship would continue. I was hoping for more. Who would want to murder him is beyond me. Where was he?"

"A jogger found him on route 117."

"I wonder what he was doing out there. He lives in South Haven. I wonder if Julie lives in Kingston. Do you think she could have killed him? Maybe she was jealous that he wanted to see other people. That's a pretty strong motive. I've seen her before. She looks like the jealous type. She told him she wanted to marry him and have his babies. She probably scared him away. I don't think he was ready to settle down."

"Did you use protection when you had sex? I hope you did. You never know these days."

"We did. He had a condom with him. Wasn't that a coincidence."

"Did he ever mention going to Tangoes strip club?"

"No. Was he there last night?"

"Yes. He paid one thousand for two prostitutes. I guess he's been saving his money for it."

"Holy shit! What a scum! I can't believe it. That's making me wish I didn't have sex with him."

"Well, that's life. Do yourself a favor next time and find out more about a guy before doing the nasty. I guess I don't have any more questions for the time being. Can you give me your phone number just in case I need to talk to you again?" Lesley found a piece of pink sticky notepaper and wrote down her phone number for George. He thanked her and went back to the elevator. He stepped in and pressed the ground floor. On his way down he chuckled to himself. Poor Lesley. At least she got some-thing out of it. She got herself some of the nasty.

He got in his car and headed for Dunkin Donuts. He parked on the side next to a red sports car. It looked similar to his car that he left at his house. He drove the squad car most of the time, but he liked his red Ferrari. He had saved his hard earned money for it. But if he was thinking of marrying Susan they would eventually need a van. Especially if they were going to have children. Right now he liked his two nephews, Jakie and Luke. They were five and seven. He liked to play ball with them. He bought them baseball mitts for their birthdays. His sister, Bonnie had a birthday party for them last month. He knew the first thing he would get his baby when the time came. He would get a baby outfit with the New England Patriots on it. That was his favorite football team. They tied with the Red Sox.

He walked inside Dunkin Donuts. There were several people working behind the counter. He asked for Julie. The other girl pointed him in the right direction.

"Julie? I'm Officer George Trent. Do you have a few minutes?"

"It's kind of busy, but I can spare a few. What's up?" Julie had curly black hair. She was tall like a bean pole. She had blush on her cheeks and was wearing dainty blue earrings. She had on a yellow uniform. Her eyes were red rimmed from crying.

"I'd like to ask you some questions about Johnston Billings. Where were you last night?"

"I saw Johnston at eight thirty last night. We talked until nine then I went back to my apartment. We broke up last night. He dumped me. He said he wanted to see other people. What a jerk."

"A girl that works with him told me you asked him to marry you. You don't do that early in the game. It scares a

man away. Johnston was murdered. Someone shot him. Do you own a gun, Julie?"

"No way. I wouldn't know what to do with a gun." She looked cautiously at him. She looked a little suspicious. George wondered if she could be covering up. She definitely looked like the jealous type. Maybe she was so upset, she followed him and shot him.

"He went to Tangoes strip club last night. Did he ever tell you about that?" George waited for her reaction.

"No. What a double jerk. He probably deserved it. I'm glad he's gone."

"Nobody deserves to be killed, Julie. Maybe he screwed around on you but that doesn't justify a murder. Death isn't good. It's a crime that happened and I plan to find out. I'll get to the bottom of things. You better not be lying to me."

"I'm not, sir. I'm an honest person."

"Did he have any brothers or sisters?"

"No. He was an only child. He has a mother, Louise. She lives in South Haven on 133 Baker St. His dad died of pancreatic cancer a few years ago."

"Thank-you, Julie. I'm sorry things didn't work out with Johnston. Maybe he wasn't the one for you. There's other fish to be had."

"I don't need a boyfriend right now. I'm getting over Johnston. Men are absolute jerks. I hate them."

"Can you jot down your phone number? I might have more questions for you later." Julie grabbed a napkin and wrote down her number. She handed it to George and he thanked her for her time. "While I'm here I guess I'll order a raspberry donut and a coffee to go." She took his order and sent him on his way with his food. He left the building and stepped into his car. He thought she seemed a little suspicious. He considered her a suspect for the time

being. She was glad he was dead. Was there something in that? She seemed to hate men. Maybe she was the killer. She could have followed Johnston and killed him out of sheer jealously. He thought of Lesley. She didn't quite look like the type that would kill. She appeared too innocent.

He ate his donut as he drove to Louise's house. He found Baker Street and parked in the driveway of her house. She lived in a yellow cape house. He saw an older woman in the yard planting flowers. She looked up when he stopped in front of her. She had been finishing deadheading her roses. She had pink ones planted next to her, but the season was done. The ones that were left were all dried up. Louise had short white hair. She wore an Icelandic sweater and black slacks. She was wearing Cole Hahn shoes. "Louise Billings? I'm Officer George Trent." She stopped what she was doing and stood up slowly.

"I've got bad knees. What brings you out here?" She looked at him nervously. She wasn't sure what was going to happen next.

"It's your son, Johnston." He was never prepared for this awful moment.

"What has he done? Is he in trouble?"

"Johnston was found dead this morning. Someone found him on route 117. He was murdered. Do you think his girlfriend, Julie could have done it? She said that he dumped her last night."

"She called me last night around nine thirty. She was hysterical. I tried to talk some sense into her but it wasn't very helpful. She wanted to find out where he went, but I couldn't tell her anything. That was between her and Johnston. I tried to keep out of it. I had to hang up on her. She kept hounding me. I can't believe someone would want to kill my baby. My poor Johnston. He was my angel. He gave me these petunia plants yesterday. It was my birthday. We had cake and ice cream. He was a nice boy. I wish he was here. I want you to find his killer and bring him or her to justice." Louise started crying and putting her hands to her face. George tried to console her.

"I'm sorry for your loss. His body is being autopsied

today. We haven't discovered the time of death yet. Did he have any friends that he liked to hang out with?"

"Just the girls at work. I think he liked one of them. He didn't go to the bars as far as I know. When his dad died he was heartbroken."

"What was he like as a child?"

"He was a good boy. He was a cub scout and he liked to play baseball."

"He was caught at Tangoes strip club last night. He paid for some hookers."

"Not my son. He wasn't like that."

"Well, my partner, Officer May found him with them. Sorry. The truth hurts. Once again I'm really sorry that it turned out this way. We'll try to get his killer. Thank-you for your time. I'll let you grieve in peace." George left and drove away. He went back to the police station. He was ready to see Susan. He missed her. He found her in the crime lab. George held her in his arms and kissed her lips. He was tender. Then he became fierce and passionate. He was needy. He wanted to have sex with her right now. His hands reached underneath her purple cotton blouse. He felt her bra and could feel her perky nipples harden. Susan ran her hands through George's hair. Their kisses became hot and heavy. George unhooked the clasp and her bra loosened. She felt his hands cupping her breasts. She moaned in ecstasy. She opened a nearby closet and nudged George into it. The shelves were filled with cleaning products. She dropped her lab coat to the floor. He unbuttoned her shirt and looked at her with utter desire. Susan fumbled with his buttons. His hairy chest was revealed. Susan's tongue grazed his chest and kissed his nipples. George unzipped his pants. He was wearing boxers with ants on them. Susan reached into his boxers and grasped hold of his penis. She rubbed it up and down. He was becoming hard quickly. She knelt down and

put his penis in her mouth. She sucked on him for five or ten minutes. She pulled out before he climaxed. George pulled down Susan's blue polka dot underwear. His hands grabbed her waist while he put his head against her pelvic region. His tongue pushed into her vagina. He gently licked her clitoris and ate her cream. Susan's hands became tangled in his thick hair. "George. George. George. I love that." Susan climaxed for him. His hands roamed over her abdomen and massaged her gently. After a few minutes he stood up and pressed his body against hers. He thrust his penis into her warm wet vagina. He sent her passionate kisses on her lips. He tasted like cherry pie. Susan grabbed his firm buns and squeezed hard. The fire of their flaming passion was hot and heated. He kissed every inch of her body like it was brand new. He couldn't get enough of her taste. She melted to his touch. His tongue grazed her neck and collarbone. She wrapped her arms around his waist. After they were all sweaty and done having sex, they got dressed and walked back into the lab. "George, you hot devil."

"So what time of death do we have for Johnston?" George got serious all of a sudden.

"He's been dead since about two fifteen am. There was no trace of fingerprints. The killer is clever and definitely wears gloves. I took fingernail clippings to see if there was any sign of a struggle. None. Zippo. There were no bruises on his body. Definitely dead by gunshot. The shot to the head killed him. The heart shot was extra. It was a .22 caliber bullet. The killer uses a 9mm gun. I was able to extract some fragments of the bullet."

Larry walked into the room. "We got a call from South Haven. Some woman's cat is stuck on her blinds. She can't get it unstuck."

"Is that something you can handle yourself? I've got some things to do here."

"Okay. I'll see you later. I'll go rescue Fluffy." He laughed and left the building.

"I'll see you later, Susan. I've got to go release Sarah. She's not our killer." Susan kissed him good-bye and went back to work.

Sarah sat on the bench. It had been a hard night being in the jail cell. She wished she was home in her soft bed. She tried not to think about Larry. After a few minutes she was surprised to see Officer Trent. He walked up to her jail cell and opened it. "You're free to go. I'd like to ask you some questions though." Sarah slowly stood and followed George into an interrogation room. She sat down in a metal chair. George sat in another chair. He pulled out the evidence from her house. "How well do you know Bernie Sanderson? We've viewed your tape of the two of you."

"He was one of the johns. He came into Tangoes a few months ago."

George pulled out the pictures of the other men. "Who are these people?"

"They were also johns."

"What do you have going on at ten am on Monday?"

"I'm going to see a dog breeder. I'm going to buy a golden retriever. I need protection."

"In the videotape, Bernie called you his black rose. What do you think he meant by that?"

"I'm not sure."

"Why are you a stripper? Why do you sell your body?"

"The money is good. I've got lots of bills. Besides, I like it. I like men looking at me. It turns me on."

"You could do lots of other things besides exposing yourself. You could stop the prostitution. There's lots of normal jobs out there. Do it soon before it's too late."

"So why am I being let off the hook? Did you realize it wasn't me?"

"Another john got murdered last night. Johnston Billings. You had sex with him last night. He was murdered while you were in jail. Someone put a black rose on him. I believe you." Sarah gasped. She was horrified. All her johns were being murdered. What could she do to stop it?

"Can I use your phone to call my sister? I need a ride to my car."

"Sure." George handed her his cell phone and left the room. Sarah punched Judy's phone number. Judy answered, "Hello?"

"Judy. It's Sarah. Can you come pick me up at the police station?"

"What are you doing there?"

"I'll explain when you get here."

"All right. I'll be there in ten or fifteen minutes." Judy hung up the phone. Sarah waited in the hallway against the yellow walls. The chairs were a little more comfortable than being in the jail cell. She was glad she was free. George came out to see her again. "Can you think of anyone who might want to threaten you?"

"I'm not sure. I come across a lot of men. It's hard to say who it could be."

"What about Bernie Sanderson."

"I don't know. He seemed like all the other johns." She knew he liked her blow jobs. He paid her well. He had given her six hundred. She didn't tell Benny. She pocketed the extra hundred.

Fifteen minutes later Judy came charging in. She saw Sarah seated in the chair. Sarah had been trying to come up with a story for Judy. She wasn't sure what she was going to tell her. She didn't want the truth getting out.

Judy was wearing a pink turtleneck and a pair of blue jeans. Her sneakers were a little dirty. Her hair was in a ponytail. Judy glared at Sarah. "So why are you here? What happened?"

"I witnessed a murder," she lied.

"Wow. What happened? "

"I was shopping at Pet Smart last night. I came out to my car and got in. Before I started up my car I looked at my side mirror. I could see a woman getting into her car. Suddenly out of nowhere a man stabbed her to death. Luckily I had my phone with me, so I called the cops. They brought me down to the station this morning for a statement. Someone composed a sketch of the man. He got away. He was wearing a mask. It was hard to tell what he looked like. The woman is dead."

"Do you think he saw you in the van? He might come after you. You weren't followed home were you?"

"No."

"That had to be scary to see someone get stabbed. I don't know what I would do. I'd probably panic." Judy hugged her sister. She was glad that Sarah was okay.

"I need to get to my car." Sarah followed Judy out of the police station. She was glad that Judy didn't know the real reason she had been here. She didn't want Judy to judge her. She wouldn't understand. Sarah was a good liar. She had been doing it for years. She could go back to stripping. On the way to her car Sarah thought about what George had said. Could she really stop stripping? It wasn't that easy. There was Benny to deal with. She couldn't handle that. What if she got beat up? She didn't want that. She was afraid of Benny. Besides

she liked the sex too much. What other job could Sarah get? She needed to pay her bills. She thought about it some more and imagined herself doing something else. Could she have a change of heart?

It was Saturday. Saturday nights at Tangoes were usually packed. Sarah looked at Judy. She didn't know that Sarah sucked men's dicks for a living. She didn't know that Sarah had experienced threesomes. What would Judy think if she knew that Sarah fucked strange men? What would she think if she found out that Sarah had kissed and fondled women? Sarah didn't want her finding out about her lifestyle. It was her dirty secret.

Judy dropped off Sarah. Judy had to go back to work. Sarah unlocked her door. She felt humiliated that Officer May had rifled through all of her things. She had wanted to chop off his dick. She arrived home and unlocked her door. She went inside and put the video back in her drawer. She was shocked. Her other videotapes were gone. The police had only seen the one of her and Bernie. They hadn't seen the other tapes. There had been one with Burt, Jeremy and Peter. If the police didn't have them where were they? Sarah wondered who had them. The person who broke into her house must have taken them. Sarah tried to think. She went into the kitchen and fixed herself a fuzzy navel. As she drank she thought of the two johns. First Teddy and then Johnston. Both were stone dead. Somehow it was something to do with her. It all had to do with the black roses. Who was sending them? Someone obviously wanted to play games with her and threaten her. She didn't like it at all. Sarah was angry, scared and pissed. How could she fight back? She didn't have the answer at the moment. She had to figure it out. Maybe she could get to the killer before the cops and find out who it was. There had to be a way. How could she tap into the killer's crazy mind. The killer was definitely sick in the head.

The person popped in the videos of Sarah in the VCR. The stranger began watching her fucking the johns. The person recognized one of the johns. The stranger had been following him for a week. The person had followed him to his job. The stranger sometimes followed him to Tangoes. The person usually sat in the back and watched Sarah perform. The person was infatuated with Sarah. She was hot. The person wanted to lick her all over and play with her body. The stranger didn't want to kill her right away. She was special. The stranger had fallen in love with her for a long time. The person had lots of pictures of her. Everything the stranger did was for Sarah. The stranger still wanted her blood on a knife. The stranger thought of Teddy and Johnston. They deserved it. The stranger thought that they were sinners. The stranger thoroughly enjoyed killing them. The person was happy to show the cops the craft of killing. It was an art form. The stranger took pictures of the dead men. The person had a darkroom. The stranger knew all about photography. The stranger followed Sarah everywhere.

The stranger knew about Judy. The person knew about little Beth. The stranger thought she was cute. It would be too bad for something to happen to her. A crying shame. The stranger continued to watch Sarah fuck the john. The stranger watched the other two videos. In one she wore a cop's uniform that she quickly stripped out of. The stranger loved her naked form. The stranger was madly in love with her.

The person picked up another bouquet of roses. The stranger grabbed a container of black acrylic paint. The stranger hummed while painting.

The stranger tried to think about who to kill next. The stranger needed to get that john out of the way. The john may have seen the stranger following him. The stranger didn't want the john talking to the cops. That Officer Trent

Nennifer Jo Fay

was butting his nose into things that weren't good. The stranger didn't want the cops on the trail.

The stranger poked a sharp knife into a picture of Sarah. The stranger loved her but knew deep in the heart that she wouldn't love back. Ultimately the stranger knew she would need to be killed. Slowly. The stranger wanted to torture her for a while.

Later that day, Julie drove home from Dunkin Donuts. She had changed out of her uniform. It was three pm. She usually got to work at five in the morning and worked until two thirty. She was tired. She began to think of Johnston. She was glad that he was dead. She thought about the gun. She had lied to the cop. She had a gun in her bedroom. It was locked in a safe under her bed. She thought about Johnston some more. He deserved it. She didn't like him dumping her. It didn't feel good. She decided that she was through with men. She didn't need them. As far as she was concerned men were no good. Men were scum. They were stupid pricks. Julie thought about that woman she had seen a while ago. She never told Johnston about her. Julie was a closet lesbian. She never told Johnston about the woman that she had fallen in love with. In fact, she still loved her. Julie had a picture of her that she tucked away in a journal. Julie was also a writer. She had gone online and contacted the woman. They emailed each other and talked a lot. Julie hadn't told her that she loved her.

Julie arrived home to her house in Kingston. It was a small apartment. All her rooms were white. Julie pulled out a painting she was working on. She was painting a picture of roses. She thought it was beautiful. She wanted to send it to the woman. She was afraid to do it. After a little while she stopped painting. She liked using acrylic paints. Her favorite color was black.

She went into the bathroom and took off her clothing. She hopped into the steamy shower. She used her rose scented soap. She found out that the woman liked the same scent. She wanted to use it too. It smelled nice. Sometimes she liked honeysuckle. Julie wished that the woman would come over. Julie wanted to have sex with her. She wanted to devour the woman with her tender loving care.

Sarah saw the postman drive by. She put down her coffee and her bowl of macaroni. She was eating a late lunch. She put on her flats and walked out to the mailbox. It was a sunny day. The beautiful rays shined upon her roses. She looked at her yellow rose bush. It needed to be deadheaded. Sarah opened her mailbox. She had several catalogs. Her Discover card statement arrived. Underneath her mail was a white envelope. There was no return address. She looked at her neighbors houses. She knew it was from the stranger. Was the stranger lurking in a bush somewhere? Just god damn waiting. The stranger was taunting her. Who the hell was it? The stranger was cunning and professional.

She opened the envelope. Several pictures fell to the ground. A black rose fell out. The sun shined upon it making it look gray. She slowly bent to retrieve the pictures. They had fallen face down. She turned them over and screamed. They were of Teddy and Johnston. They were small black and white photos and the men were extremely dead. Teddy's dead naked body taunted her. There was another picture stuck in the envelope. She pulled it out and began to cry. The crystalline tears slipped down her cheeks. It was a photo of Judy. Her beloved sister. The stranger was aiming close. Was Judy going to be in danger? Would Beth be motherless? Did the killer know where Judy lived? She needed to warn Judy.

If she did she may have to reveal her secret life. Was she ready for that? Prostitute revealed in big lettering. She didn't want to imagine Judy's face. No. She couldn't. She walked into the house and retrieved her phone. She called George. He picked up on the third ring. "Hello."

"Hi. This is Sarah Fisher. I received some photos in the mail from the killer. There was a photo of my sister, Judy. She's still alive as far as I know but I'm afraid that she is going to be in danger. Can you help her?"

"I suppose we could have a car watch her house in the evenings. Would that make you feel better? What were some of the other photos?"

"There was one of Teddy and Johnston. Both were dead."

"Maybe the killer develops photos. If the stranger sent them to be developed they would get caught. Our killer is very smart. Be careful."

"Maybe a florist shop can track the rose purchases. The stranger has to get them somewhere."

"I'll start looking into that. I'm not sure what we'll come up with but it's worth a shot."

"Thank-you." Sarah hung up the phone. She went into the living room and wrote some poetry in her book. After a few poems she thought again of Judy. She wondered if the killer knew where she worked. A little while later Sarah checked her emails. She chatted with a few other women a lot. It was great to establish some friends outside of work.

At eight pm Sarah got in her car to go visit Judy and Beth. Judy had Beth tonight. Henry got her from Tuesday to Thursdays. They lived in the same town so the bus knew to pick up Beth at both places.

Once she arrived she saw Judy's car in the driveway. Across the street she saw a squad car. She felt relieved and silently thanked Officer Trent. She went inside. Beth was reading a Judy Blume book titled Superfudge. She was wearing a plaid shirt and polka dot pants. She had on bunny slippers.

"Hi, pumpkin. How are you?"

"Fine, Aunt Sarah. Guess what?"

"What?"

"You're stuck with it. Ha! Ha!"

"Silly."

"Guess what though. Really. I'm not fooling."

"What?"

"Mom said we could go pick out a puppy next weekend."

"Oh. That's exciting," Sarah said enthusiastically."Guess what?"

"What?" she asked with calm curiosity.

"I'm going to look at puppies on Monday. I'm going to get one too. Can you help me think of names?"

"How about Spunky."

"That sounds neat. Maybe."

"Cool."

"Where's your mom?"

"She's cleaning up in the kitchen."

Sarah went into the kitchen and saw Judy. She was busy doing dishes. Sarah startled her and she dropped a plastic cup on the floor. She picked it up with soapy hands.

"Hi, Sarah. What are you up to?"

"I might take a trip out to Pet Smart pretty soon. I'm

looking at some puppies on Monday. It will be good to get some protection."

"Yeah. In case that guy you saw stab that woman shows up on your doorstep. I had nightmares just thinking about it."

"Hey, remember me telling you about those black roses?"

"Yes. Why? Is the person still sending them?"

"Yes."

"That's creepy. Did you call the cops?"

"Yes. There were no fingerprints. The stranger uses gloves."

"Watch out, Sarah." Sarah wanted to tell her about the pictures. She couldn't do it.

"I watched Mrs. Doubtfire this afternoon."

"That's a good movie. You might want to involve yourself with the local church. Maybe you could meet a nice guy there. Just a suggestion."

"Are you trying to get me hooked up?"

"Do you still miss Justin?"

"That was a long time ago, Judy."

"I know." Judy said glumly. "But you haven't met a nice man since him."

Sarah thought about Justin. It had indeed been a long time. There was no turning back. She thought of Susie. What would Judy think if she knew that Sarah had fondled Susie? She didn't want to tell her. She didn't want to tell her about the women she emailed.

"Did you find out who the woman was that got stabbed?" Sarah almost forgot she had told a lie. The invisible woman.

"No. The cops didn't tell me. I should get going to Pet Smart before it closes. I think I'll at least buy some doggie toys. So I hear you and Beth are going to get a dog."

"Yup. Next Saturday we're going to look at some pug dogs."

"Fun. Well I'll see you later."

Sarah left the kitchen and walked out of the house. It was starting to rain and the roads were wet. The sunny day was long gone. She got in her car and drove to Pet Smart. She walked to the dog section. There were lots of toys to choose from. Sarah picked up a blue bouncy ball and a fluffy chew toy. She put a few bones in her basket. She also decided she needed a dog book so she could learn about Spunky. Beth picked a good name. Beth was going to have lots of fun with Spunky.

Sarah got to the checkout and paid for her items. There was a person behind her holding a kitten magazine. She smiled and then left with her bags.

The stranger watched Sarah walk to her car. The person threw the kitten magazine in the back seat of the Porsche. The stranger really didn't want a kitten. It was just something to hold while watching Sarah. The stranger followed Sarah to Tangoes. The stranger waited outside for a little bit. The stranger didn't want to go into the bar right away. The stranger wrote another noteand got out of the car. The person put it on Sarah's car, left a black rose on the windshield and walked away.

At ten pm Sarah walked into Tangoes. She got into the dressing room and changed into a nurse outfit. Tonight she was Nurse Betty. She stood up and was about to go on stage when Benny waltzed in. He grabbed her waist and pushed up her skirt. He pushed her onto the floor and began fucking her in the ass. She cried out in pain. It hurt. Benny held her hips and moaned and groaned. Sarah cried some more. When he was done, he left the room.

Sarah gained back her composure and fixed her uniform. She looked at herself in the mirror. She wondered if Benny could be the killer. She wasn't sure about anybody now. She was glad that Judy was safe.

Sarah left the room and walked out on the stage. There were red and blue stage lights. She sang and danced erotically. She felt sultry tonight. Suddenly she whipped off her uniform and left it on the floor. She wore her edible underwear tonight and she had black tassels on her tits. She danced and slid around the pole for a little while. Then she leaned against a chair that was on the stage. She sat down on the chair and arched her back and pulled a string. Water splashed on her. She got up and danced some more. She heard lots of whistling in the audience. She slid across the stage and landed near several men. They stood up and started fondling her. They stuck money in her g-string. She gave them several kisses. She stepped off the stage and sat on a man's lap. His hands wrapped around her back and he grabbed her butt. Then his hands grabbed and pulled off her tassels. She threw them on the stage. Then his mouth sucked on one of her tits. He put more money in her g-string. She pushed him away and started giving other men lap dances. There was a person in the back with a camera. She went over to the person and grabbed the camera. "Want a closer look?" She gave the person a lap dance and rubbed her body all over the stranger. Then she got up and gave some lap dances to other men. Soon she got back

on stage and started dancing more. Susie was also dancing. They danced together sometimes. The men found it erotic to watch them.

Later Sarah was back in the dressing room. She had received one hundred twenty five in tips. Benny came in and collected some of the money. She didn't like that. She put on her nurse uniform and walked up the red carpeted stairs to room number seven. She paused outside the door. It was the same room Teddy was murdered in. She was going back in.

She opened the door and walked inside. Two men were waiting for her. One was the man with the beard and the other was a younger man with long black hair. He was tall and muscular. He was wearing a purple dress shirt and black slacks.

The man with the beard was wearing a black tee shirt and blue jeans. The man with the beard stood up and walked towards Sarah. His hairy hands grabbed her and he began pulling away the uniform. It quickly fell to the floor. He pushed her on the bed and undid his shirt and stripped down to his boxers. Then he leaned upon her and began to penetrate his dick into her vagina. He fucked her hard and his hands cupped her breasts.

Meanwhile the younger man had stripped down and he began to fondle and lick her breasts while the other guy continued fucking her. When he was done Sarah got on her knees and began sucking the younger guy's dick. Her hands held his pelvis. He moaned and cried out. His hands wound their way through her hair. She sucked on him hard and slow. Her tongue glided up to the tip of his dick and then sucked him deep again. He climaxed and she ate his sperm. Then he pulled her up on him. She wrapped her legs around him and he fucked her. After he was done he licked her pussy and ate her underwear. He devoured her cream and she moaned. His

Sarah left and walked to her van. She saw the black rose and the note on her window. She chose not to read them tonight. She turned on her windshield wipers and let them fall off the car. She thought about the stranger with the camera. The stranger was a creep. Could the stranger have been a murderer? She drove through several neighborhoods. The roads were dark. It had stopped raining. She pulled into her driveway. It was three am. She got out of her car and grabbed her Gucci purse. It had been expensive but worth it. Her house was dark. She unlocked her door and walked inside. She tossed her purse on the loveseat and was ready to turn on the light. Suddenly out of she felt strong hands grab her neck. She struggled and tried to breath for a few minutes. After a few minutes her attacker loosened the grip and started punching her in the face and in the stomach. She tried to scream but a hand muffled her screams. "Cry out and I'll kill you."

It was dark and she couldn't see anything. What little sliver of moonlight that shined in wasn't enough to make out anything. She tried to kick her attacker but the stranger was too strong. The stranger roughed her up some more and threw some more punches to her body. She looked up at the stranger for a moment and thought she saw a mask. It was black and she couldn't see a face.

After fifteen minutes the stranger stopped attacking her and let her lie on the floor. Her lip was bleeding. She cried, "Why? Why me?"

"My black rose," the stranger said. She couldn't tell if it was a man or a woman. The voice was muffled. The stranger dropped something light on her and left the house. The door was left wide open.

Ten minutes passed. Sarah could hear several cars going by. Probably people heading to work or out late. Sarah cried.

She slowly tried to move. Her body hurt so bad. It felt like someone had taken a hammer to her and gutted her out. What was she, one of those candy pigs? It felt like her ribs were broken. Slowly she tried to get up. She sat up. Her legs were scratched up. She was bleeding. Then she saw the black roses. The stranger had tossed them on her. There were a dozen on her lap. Those fucking black roses.

Was it Bernie? He was the only one who called her my black rose. She knew where he lived. She stood up and staggered to the loveseat. She grabbed her purse and pulled out her car keys. She checked her purse for the little pistol. The cops hadn't seen it. She shut her door and locked it. Then she limped and staggered for her car. She opened the door and slowly sat down. She waited a minute before starting the car. Her chest hurt. She put the keys in the ignition and drove out of the driveway. She headed to South Haven. Once she got to Bernie's neighborhood she drove slowly. She parked a few blocks away from his apartment. She limped down the street. There were lots of trees and bushes. She imagined being mugged again on the dark street. Nobody would come to her rescue because it was so late. Nobody was out at three thirty am. Except for the homeless. She didn't like walking through his neighborhood. All the apartments were run down.

Finally she got to his apartment building. She found his floor. It was dark inside and the silence was deadly. She leaned against the door and caught her breath. She tried to live through her pain. She had to be ready for Bernie. What if he had his gun ready? She dug through her purse and found her credit card. She jimmied it into Bernie's door. After a minute the door opened. Ever so slowly she walked through his mudroom. She walked into his small kitchen. Bernie was probably upstairs sleeping. She went into the living room.

Maybe she would find some evidence. She walked into the room and searched for a light. Immediately she fell over something and fell upon the carpet. She fumbled around and discovered his black leather couch. There was an end table with a lamp on it. She reached up and turned on the light. The lamp was a naked lady and the light switch was on the tits.

She opened his drawer on the end table and found a box of cigars. He smoked. She turned around and let out a fierce scream.

The carpet was blue and it was stained with a pool of blood. Next to the blood was Bernie. She had stumbled over him. He was naked and severely dead. She looked in horror at his body. The word sinner had been tattooed on his stomach. He had a bullet through his head. It also looked like he had been strangled as he had marks on his neck. How long had he been this way? Then she saw the black rose lying on the floor. The killer had struck again. The killer wasn't Bernie. She was shocked. She turned around the room. She shouldn't be here. It was wrong. But she had wanted to strike back at Bernie. She sat down on the couch and began to cry. She had fucked Bernie and now he was dead. It's like everyone she came across was dying. Was it all her fault? She pulled out a cigarette from her purse and lit it. She began to smoke. She was addicted and couldn't stop. Could she stop stripping? She felt really dirty after fucking those two men. It was wrong and she knew it. She had to find a way in her heart to stop. Before it was too late. She looked at Bernie's dead body. Death was all around her. She cried again and the warm tears slowly trickled down her cheeks. Her body still hurt but the blood on her legs had dried up. She turned on his large television. There was nothing on but she liked the noise. It broke the silence and cut like a knife. She dabbed her cigarette into his ashtray. His ashtray was in the

shape of a lady's ass. Nice. What a pervert he was. Now he was a dead one. Shit. She sat there while her nerves escalated. Next to his television there was a poster of a woman's pussy. His curtains were yellow. Next to the television there was a stack of DVDS sitting on a shelf. One was called Sin City. Another was Shoot Em Up with Clive Owen. Both were probably sex movies. Shoot Em Up had a hooker in it.

Finally she discovered a phone in the drawer of the coffee table. She waited. What was she going to say to the police? She had broken into his apartment. How was that going to look? She had to report his death. She couldn't just leave him there. For all she knew he could have been dead for several days.

She pulled out Officer Trent's phone number. He had given it to her after he found out she was innocent.

After the third ring he picked up. "Hello. Who is this?" It was four fifteen am.

"It's Sarah Fisher. Sorry to wake you. I'm at Bernie Sanderson's house. He's dead. He's been murdered."

"Okay. Damn. I thought he may be the killer. I guessed wrong. I'll be over in fifteen to twenty minutes. Don't go anywhere. I need to know what happened." He hung up the phone. George reached over and kissed Susan. "Honey, I've got to go to South Haven. A suspect has been murdered."

"Okay. I love you."

"I love you. Keep the bed warm."

"By the time you come back I'll be making coffee. I bought Dunkin Donuts yesterday."

George got up and put on a plaid shirt and a pair of blue jeans. He tied his sneakers and left the room. Once downstairs he called Larry to let him know. Larry told him he would meet him there. George grabbed his notepad and tape recorder. Then he reached for his car keys. They were resting on the mahogany table. It had been given to him

by his mother. George's mother was married and lived in Kingston. George also lived in Kingston. He had a nice cape cod house. He had saved his money and bought a house. Susan lived in an apartment. He thought of Susan as he drove to South Haven. He felt like he was ready to settle down. Maybe in a few months at Christmastime he would buy her a ring and ask her to marry him. Maybe he would put the ring in a cupcake like in the Little Rascals. When he got down on one knee she would know.

The stranger went to bed dreaming of Sarah. The stranger cried. The person really didn't want to hurt her. But she hadn't given him a choice. She was sinning. The stranger didn't like sinners, but she was special. The stranger had power over her. The stranger wanted to hurt her. It was part of the stranger. The person dreamed of her giving that lap dance. The stranger loved her body touching. It had felt great. The stranger wanted more of her. The person had to have her again. The stranger planned on going to Tangoes and decided to pay for her time. The stranger cried at thinking that now she was suffering. The stranger wanted her to be different. Sarah was special. The stranger dreamed of caressing her lovely breasts. The stranger wanted to eat her cream. The stranger was having some sexual fantasies. The stranger still loved Sarah. The stranger wanted to fuck her hard. The stranger thought of Bernie. He was in the way. He had to die. And same with that bearded man. He had die too. The stranger had only wanted to teach Sarah a lesson. Love hurts.

Fifteen minutes later George arrived in South Haven. He found 117 Torrence Street and parked the car. Larry was waiting outside the apartment. He lived in South Haven on South Street so he was fifteen minutes closer.

"Hi. Such a late hour. It was four fifteen when she called me. Let's go in and find out what happened."

Both men walked up the steps and went to Bernie's apartment. They met Sarah in the living room. They saw her sitting on the couch. They looked at the television. She was watching Shoot Em Up. The wondered why she popped that in the DVD player.

They took a look at her. "What happened to you?" asked George. Sarah had a black eye and some bruises on her cheeks and her nurse uniform had blood on it. They saw her scratched up legs.

"I got home to my house and three am. When I got inside my mudroom someone with a mask attacked me. I might have broken ribs."

"Why didn't you call 911 and go to the hospital? Your neck has some bruises too. Did the person try to strangle you?"

"Yes. The stranger mostly punched and kicked me."

"Why are you here?" asked Larry.

"My attacker called me my black rose. I thought it was Bernie. I wanted to get revenge. Maybe find some evidence."

"That was dangerous and stupid. Leave the investigating to us. You realize if he had been the murderer he could have been armed and dangerous." George looked at Bernie. Shot dead in the head just like Teddy and Johnston. "Look at the bruises on his neck. He was strangled too. I wonder if that was after the bullet. Must have been. He's got scratches on his hands. He must have put up a fight. Maybe the bullet

didn't kill him right away. He must have been strangled to quiet him." George turned on the cassette recorder.

"How did you get in?" Larry asked.

"I used a credit card. It performs miracles. I walked in, went in his kitchen, then the living room. It was dark. I tripped over his body and fell." Larry looked in her purse. He pulled out her pistol.

"Do you have a license for this?"

"Yes. Do you need proof?"

"That would be good. You can find it and bring it to the station tomorrow. Or actually later this morning. So far you have three guns and no license. That's a crime until you show proof of your license. " Larry looked at her nurse uniform. What a devil she must me. He smirked. He wished she could give him another blow job.

Larry looked at Bernie. He saw the word sinner. "I'd say our murderer has a thing against sinners. I'm wondering why you was spared." He studied Sarah for a moment. Here she was again at the scene of a crime with a gun in her purse. "I'm going to take your gun. You can get your guns back when you bring in your license."

"Are you suggesting that I'm a sinner? Admit it, you've sinned too. You were sinning while I sucked your penis. You're lucky I didn't bite it off. When you're in the bathroom jerking off you're sinning. You like to jerk off don't you. I know men like you. You liked being at Tangoes didn't you? I've got nice honkers. You'd like to see them wouldn't you. Would you like to see what's under my uniform? Would you like to see what's left of my edible underwear? Oh wait you already saw them in my drawer. Did you eat one? Or are you waiting to lick the one off my crotch? Wait, you investigated my whole house, you jerk. What did you think about my video? Did it make you hard? What size is your dick?" Sarah asked sarcastically.

Larry looked at her. His face turned cherry red. Could she read his mind? He didn't tell her that it was her that he thought of when he was jerking off. "I'm not going to tell you what size my dick is. By the way, watch your mouth. I'm a cop."

"I sucked it. Your dick is small." Larry glared at her. George glanced at Larry. He didn't want to know what had happened. When did Larry get her to suck his penis? Did he do something illegal?

"Hey, Larry! What did you do, man? Let's get back to the investigation. I don't want to know what the size of your nuts are." George found an answering machine and played it. Bernie's boss had left two messages wondering why he didn't show up for work. He didn't show up for work Friday or Saturday. "Okay. Bernie has been dead for at least two days." George went into the kitchen . He opened the cupboard. He found boxes of Honeycomb and Corn Pops. Bernie liked sugar cereal. There was also a mug that said World's Biggest Dick. George wondered in an ex girlfriend gave him it. Why would he keep a cup like that? On the other hand, maybe he had a big dick. He thought of asking Sarah but refrained from doing so.

George scratched his nose. He had an itch. At least he didn't pick his nose. He hadn't done that since he was little. His mother made him eat soap after that. Since that day he picked his nose in privacy. His mother didn't know.

George opened the refrigerator. There was a case of beer and a gallon of milk. It was Hood. Also there was a three day old pizza on the counter. Three slices were left. So pizza was probably his last meal. George found the light switch and turned it on. Bernie's curtains were olive green. There were notes on the table. One said Call Mom. The other said Dentist one pm, Tuesday. Did he miss it? Or did it already happen?

George looked around for a sign of a rolodex or a little black book. Didn't all men have a little black book? Especially men who went to Tangoes. Finally he found it on a bookshelf. It was red and small. He found a phone number for Jeanne Blackmore. There was another for Libby Blackmore. One of them had to be the mother. The other was probably a sister. It was too early to call them. There was a phone number for his boss, Jason. Bernie worked for The Auto body as a mechanic. There was a phone number for Ava Peabody. Maybe a girlfriend. Or an ex-girlfriend. There were other phone numbers. He would ask the mother in a few hours. Maybe a lot of numbers were relatives. Once he talked to the mother or the sister they could pass on the bad news.

George called the forensics team. They would be there shortly to investigate the crime scene and eventually bag the body and take it to the funeral home. Susan would wake up and head there to autopsy the body. George inspected the coffee maker. There was a fresh pot of coffee. It was full. Bernie didn't get a chance to drink it. There was a bag of onion bagels on the counter. A half eaten bag of wheat bread was next to it. His container of cream cheese was left on the counter. Did he get interrupted at breakfast on Thursday? He'd have to ask Jason if he had the day off. He was beginning to think that the killer came in and stopped Bernie's day cold. George was dealing with a crafty cold blooded serial killer. George wanted to catch the killer really bad. They had to find a breakthrough with evidence soon. There had to be something to go on. If only they could find the killer's blood to match DNA. Then they could nail the person. Maybe Bernie's fingernail clippings would prove some results. One could only hope.

George walked down the hall to Bernie's bedroom. His king size bed was large and brown. The headboard had a

large mirror on it. Bernie liked to view himself and women. There were condoms left out on the shelf. There was a phone number on it. It said Susie. He picked it up and put it in the telephone book.

He opened the drawer to his night stand. Bernie had a rather large knife in it. It looked medieval. He found more knives in the closet. Bernie had a knife fetish. He found nothing else of interest in the bedroom and went back to the living room. He got on his phone and called an ambulance. He got off the phone and looked at Sarah. "An ambulance is coming for you. You need to get your ribs checked."

"Thank-you." Sarah liked Officer Trent. He seemed like a nice man. She couldn't say the same for Larry. Larry looked like he wanted to fuck her. A few minutes later the forensics team arrived. They started checking for fingerprints, taking photographs and searching the area for trace evidence. Hopefully they would discover something. George prayed.

Ten minutes later the ambulance arrived and the medical team helped Sarah out of the apartment and into the ambulance. She hadn't been in one since she was a little girl. Once she broke her leg on the ski slope and she got put on a stretcher and into an ambulance. That was when she was twelve years old. It seemed like forever.

Larry held onto the pistol. He turned off the movie. It was in the middle of a raunchy sex scene and guns were being fired everywhere. He could see why it was called Shoot Em Up. "That's three johns murdered. All of them fucked Sarah. The person could have killed Sarah but didn't. Maybe the person wants to spare her. Why? Do you think the killer is saving her for last? Maybe the person likes her. It could be a john. Someone that is fascinated with her."

"I think the person wants her to know that all the johns are being killed. The question is when will the killer be

done? We need to catch the killer before too many more deaths occur."

"It's definitely a serial killer. The person doesn't stop at one. The killer enjoys it too much."

"Let's get to the station. Susan should be there in about twenty minutes. Then I'll start calling on people. It's almost six am. It's time to get more answers." They left the forensics team to do their job.

By six am they were at the station. Larry went to the break room for some coffee and donuts. George went to see Susan. They kissed each other passionately for a few minutes. "I brought you some coffee," she said. "They're going to have Bernie at the funeral home in an hour. I'll head over soon. I'll see you later. How was the crime scene?"

"He was shot in the head and strangled. There may have been a sign of a struggle. Maybe you can find some evidence later. We need that break."

"It sounds gruesome. So far there has been nothing to indicate anything. I kept the bed warm for you. We'll make up for lost time tonight." Susan grabbed her keys and left.

Back in his office, George called Jeanne Blackmore. "Hello?" a woman answered.

"Is this Jeanne Blackmore?" He waited a minute before hearing an answer.

"Yes."

"This is Officer George Trent. Are you the mother of Bernie Blackmore?"

"No. I'm his sister. Why? What has happened? Has he been arrested?"

"He's been murdered. When did you see him last?"

"It was last week. My mom had a get together."

"Did Bernie have any enemies? Has he been arrested before? "

"I don't know if he had any enemies. He's been arrested once for beating up Ava. She's his ex-girlfriend."

"I saw her phone number. How long ago did they break up?"

"A few months ago. They got together again after he got out of jail. She missed him. I can't believe he's dead. My mother is going to be upset. Let me tell her."

"Where do you work?"

"I'm a receptionist for a dentist office. I work in Kingston."

"How old was Bernie?"

"He was thirty four."

"Did you know he went to Tangoes strip club?"

"Yes. He told me last week."

"How often do you think he went?"

"I don't know. Maybe several times."

"He paid for a prostitute named Sarah. I found a phone number for a Susie."

"I've never heard of her."

"Thank-you for your time. I'm sorry for your loss." George hung up the phone. He sipped more of his coffee. It was getting cold so he went into the break room and heated it in the microwave. He grabbed a cheese Danish. Lucy had brought them in as a treat. Sometimes she baked brownies or made cookies. She was a dear to have around. She was married and lived in South Haven. She had a few grandchildren. Her daughter usually let her have them for part of the weekends. He went back into the office and played his cassette recorder. He thought of Sarah. He hoped that she was alright. She was a very lucky girl. He really hoped that she would take his advice and stop stripping. She was a really pretty girl and he thought it was too bad she had to resort to selling her body like that. She could get a disease. He still couldn't believe that she had sucked Larry's penis. He wondered if he forced her to do it. For Larry's sake he better hope that she doesn't press charges. Larry could be in deep muck. George thought that Larry needed to try to settle down and find himself a nice woman. Maybe he was a little on the wild side. George wondered about his partner. How much did he really know him? He did like Susan sucking on his penis, but that was different. They were dating and pleasuring each other. He wanted to

marry her. He knew that she was the one. His sister would be happy for him. He needed to see his nephews again soon. Maybe they would all sit down and watch Teenage Mutant Ninja Turtles. That was a fun movie. Luke was that for Halloween. George and Susan liked to see all the kids dressed up that night. They usually got rid of lots of candy. George usually saved a few of the Reeses peanut butter cups. One Halloween there was a robbery at a local mom and pop store. The person was dressed up as the Mad Hatter and he had a gun. They caught the guy and he did some time in the slammer. That was a night to remember arresting that turkey.

Next he called Susie. She answered, "Hello? Who is this?"

"This is Officer George Trent. Is this Susie?"

"Yes."

"Bernie Blackmore is dead. He's been murdered. Can you meet me at Café Blanche for a cup of coffee so I can ask you some questions?" George wondered if Bernie beat her up too. He was a little surprised to hear that he was abusive. Although when George had interviewed him he thought he could be a rough kind of guy. The man hadn't shaved in three or four days. Plus he lied to George. He must have been a troublemaker. George wondered what his childhood had been like. Maybe there was a history of abuse. Maybe he should call Libby Blackmore and find out. He was curious. That's one of the reasons why he was a really good cop. He always wanted to get to the bottom of things. It was his nature. He loved reading mysteries when he was a teenager. It fascinated him. There were all these puzzles to solve. He was good at solving them.

"Sure." There was a brief silence on the other end of the line. He wondered what Susie was thinking.

"How about in twenty minutes. It's important."

"Okay." She hung up the phone. Soon he would find out who Susie was. Maybe she was an old flame. Or she could be someone completely new. Maybe Bernie had a new woman in his life. He wondered if that made Ava jealous. He needed to meet her too. Maybe there was a motive. George wondered what made people tick. He tried to get inside the mind of the killer. There must be something special about Sarah. Maybe the killer loves her. But why would the killer try to hurt her? Maybe the killer wants to make it painful for her.

Twenty minutes later he got to Café Blanche and waited. After a few minutes a woman with brown hair approached him. She had blue eyes. She was wearing a low cut peach top that showed her ample cleavage. She also was wearing a very short skirt and black stilettos. She was about five foot four. He could see why Bernie liked her. Maybe Susie was promiscuous. Bernie seemed to like that.

"I'm Susie Lockhart." She looked at George cautiously.

"I'm Officer George Trent. Please have a seat." He had two coffees waiting. "I hope you like cream and sugar."

"Sure. How was he murdered?" She sat down across from him and sipped her coffee. She crossed her legs and her stiletto grazed George's leg. He was startled and moved his foot.

"He was shot and strangled. When was the last time you saw him?"

"Wednesday night at his house." She nervously pulled back a strand of her hair and looked the other way. There was a young couple sitting a few tables away. The girl was staring at Susie. Susie winked at her. George caught it and grinned. Why would she do that?

"Was he alive when you left him?"

"I didn't kill him." She scowled. She gave him a dirty look.

"I didn't say that you did. What did you do with him on Wednesday?" He wanted to know what Susie was all about. So far she could be a suspect. Maybe she was the last person to see him alive. Maybe she was there when he was killed. Maybe the killer had an accomplice. George was trying to think of everything. He needed more answers. Clues were necessary.

"I had sex with him. Off the clock." Her stiletto rubbed against his pants again.

"What do you mean?"

"I'm a prostitute and a stripper." George suddenly realized that she worked at Tangoes. She must know Sarah.

"Did he pay for your time?"

"Yes. But I started seeing him once in a while too."

"Did Johnston also pay for you?"

"He did. He paid for Sarah and I."

"At the same time?" George looked incredulous.

Susie grinned. "Yeah. He was kinky. He wanted to see Sarah and I getting off on each other. He liked that kind of thing. Admit it, you like seeing women kissing each other. You must think about us having sex and rubbing our bodies all over each other." She laughed and pushed her stiletto higher. George smiled at her and figured right now she was harmless. He watched her wink at the girl again.

"Did you like that?"

"We had fun. Sarah and I have a history. Ask her sometime."

"Are you a lesbian?"

"Yes. I also was with Bernie once in a while. Are you aroused?"

George blushed. "I have a girlfriend. Is Sarah a lesbian?"

"She might be. I've got a girlfriend, Betty now. I didn't really love Bernie but we had sex once in a while. Betty was okay with that. She doesn't mind that I fuck men for a living. The money is really good. I've got lots of bills."

" Sounds like you're in the same boat as Sarah. Do you do drugs?"

"Sometimes. Betty does too. I like Betty a lot. She's sexy."

"So you prefer women?"

"I do. She's much more gentle than some of the men."

"But you don't mind me? Did you ever go to Johnston's house?"

"No. I only fucked him once. It's too bad he's dead. So you've got a serial killer on your hands. I hope the person gets caught."

"The killer is smart. So far there are no fingerprints. Did Bernie ever beat you up? Do you think Bernie had enemies?"

"Not that I know of. Am I free to go? And he never beat me."

"Sure. I guess that's it for now. Are you working tonight?"

"Yes. Sarah is too."

"She's at the hospital right now. She got attacked by the killer at three am. She's very lucky. The person chose not to kill her. Be careful. You know Sarah. You could be a target. It seems like everyone is connected to her."

"In what condition is she?" Susie suddenly looked really worried.

"She might have some broken ribs."

"I'll let Benny know." Susie got up and left. George finished his coffee and left for the police station. He decided he would pay a visit to the police station later. Suddenly his phone rang. It was Lucy. "What's up?"

"There's been another murder. There's a man dead in his car near Tangoes."

"Thank-you, Lucy."

"Larry is already there."

"Okay. I'll leave right now."

Julie was behind the counter at Dunkin Donuts. It was busy this morning. She had had a busy night last night. She went to the woman's house to see her. She had parked on the side of the street for a while and finally got up the nerve to go in. When she left she was very happy. The woman looked hurt when she left. Julie wondered if the woman loved her too. She hoped and prayed. Maybe things would finally go her way. She didn't really want to hurt her but Julie was upset. She got that way when she loved someone. She had felt the same way for Johnston, but he broke her heart. It was always that way. People were breaking her heart. Sometimes it turned her into something violent. She remembered back to her childhood when her sister caught her torturing a fallen bird. Her sister told her that she was sick. She had been curious to see what the bird looked like inside.

She served a young guy his hot chocolate and donuts. He smiled at her. She scowled at him. She really didn't like men anymore. All she wanted was that woman. She was patient. She could wait for her. She would come around. One of the other girls, Sandy was busy putting the donuts in the boxes. Sandy asked her once if she was gay. Julie told her no. She was kind of embarrassed about it. She didn't want the world to know it. She wasn't ready to come out of the closet. She kind of liked girls when she was a teenager. Once she had a wet dream about having sex with her sister. Sometimes she would open the door ajar when her sister was taking a shower. She would watch her naked form behind the glass. Once her sister caught her and asked her what she was doing. Julie covered up and said she was coming in to brush her teeth. She also had a secret crush on one of the cheerleaders. She would follow her around school like a lost puppy. Once they were in the girls locker room together. They were all getting dressed. Julie watched her strip down to her bra. The cheerleader took it off in front of her and

took off her pink underpants. Julie had looked at her creamy white breasts and her perky little nipples. She wanted to suck them. Then the girl went into the shower. Julie had watched her naked body walk away. She had been aroused. She never dared to confront the girl about her feelings. She was ashamed of them. She had fantasies about having sex with her. It was always erotic. Sweet desires.

Now she wasn't that way. She felt stronger and she knew she had strong desires for the woman. Things were different now. She was more sure of herself.

Jeanne Blackmore drove over to her mother's house in Kingston. She figured it was better to tell her in person. Jeanne's eyes were red. She had jade green eyes and curly blond hair. She had a heart shaped face. She was wearing a yellow sweater and a black sweatshirt. She had on blue jeans. She was supposed to be at Dr. Johnson's office in an hour for work. She had to try to hold it together. She already missed her brother a lot. Jeanne was thirty two. She was just a few years younger than Bernie was. It was awful that he was gone. She had always loved his sense of humor. She thought of the stripper he paid money for. Bernie had got himself into trouble again. Now someone had wanted him dead. She couldn't imagine anyone killing her brother. She arrived at her mother's house. Today the sun was out but it was cold. It was a sign that winter was soon to be here.

Libby lived in a red painted ranch house. There were several lilac trees near the windows. Her husband was dead. He had died a few years ago from lung cancer. In a way it was a blessing that he was dead. He used to beat up Libby and the kids. Jeanne and Bernie had many memories of him lashing out at them. It hadn't been a really happy childhood. Once Libby threatened to leave him and he beat her really bad. She could have been killed.

Jeanne found Libby in the kitchen. She was finishing up the breakfast dishes. Libby had long gray hair with traces of blond hair. Her eyes were green and her complexion was red. She had high blood pressure and diabetes. She was on medicine for both. She was doing okay with it. Libby was wearing a brown wool sweater and gray slacks. She had on Icelandic socks. Libby liked to knit in her spare time. Libby was retired. She used to be a schoolteacher. "Hi, honey. How are you?"

"Mommy, I've got bad news."

"What?"

"Bernie has been murdered." Libby put her soapy hands to her face and started to cry. They hugged each other for a while. It was finally sinking in that he was really gone and he was never coming back. There would be no more family gatherings with the three of them. Now it was just Jeanne and her mom. Fortunately Jeanne was married. They had two children. Jasper and Geneva. There would still be some family but it wouldn't be the same without Bernie.

"Who on earth could have killed him? Why my son?"

"I don't know mom. The police are trying to get the killer."

"I hope they catch him and keep him in jail forever. Whoever it is deserves the death penalty." Libby was furious. Bernie didn't deserve death. It was impossible that he was gone.

"Do you want me to stay with you? I could take a personal day. They would understand."

"Okay, dear. We should be together today." Jeanne pulled out a coffee cake and they had some comfort food. It was quiet without Bernie. Bernie would usually make them laugh for hours. They cried some more. Later both women's eyes were swollen and red rimmed.

George parked the squad car across from Tangoes. Larry was investigating and the forensics team was already working the scene. George stepped out of the car. It was cold so he grabbed his tweed sports coat.

There was a black Volvo at the crime scene. George looked inside. There was a naked man with a beard inside the car. A black rose was taped to his stomach. He was a little chunky. He had been shot in the head like the others. His eyes were staring into nothing. The killer might not have had time to write sinner on him. The man had a hairy chest and he had a hairy penis. There was no sign if any clothing near him. The killer had taken it. Larry got out a Polaroid

camera and began snapping pictures. Then he went inside to Tangoes to talk to Benny.

Larry discovered Benny in his office. "Hi. I saw all the cars across the street. What happened?"

"Another murder. Do you recognize this man?"

"Morbid. He was one of the johns. He paid for Sarah. There was another man with him." Larry looked at Benny for a few minutes. He was wearing a shirt that said Fuck You. He was smoking a cigar.

"Do you know this man's name? What about the other man?"

"His name was Harold Baker. The other man I'm not sure of. The other man was younger. He was tall and had a ponytail. I think his hair was black. I had never seen him before. Both men paid for Sarah for two hours. I had a bunch of girls working last night. Susie was here. I've got another girl named Rebecca and another named Louisa."

"Wow. Sarah was busy. I bet she sucked a lot of penis."

"She usually does." Benny said with a smile. "You should try her sometime."

"Oh, I have. She's already given me a blow job."

"Did you give her money? If you did she hasn't told me about it. The bitch."

"I didn't have to pay her. I'm a police officer. I have the power." Larry grinned. "So where did Harold live?"

"In Kingston."

"Thanks, Benny. I'll be back if I have more questions." Larry went back to the scene.

"His name is Harold Baker. He lives in Kingston. He and another guy paid for Sarah last night. Two hours worth of blow jobs. Incredible."

"You probably wish it was you, huh?" George gave him a wary eyeball. "So what did you do to get her to suck your penis. Was she willing?"

"You bet." He lied. Larry knew that he could get in a lot of trouble for what he did. He was a little nervous and hoped that Sarah wouldn't do anything. Maybe she kind of liked it and wouldn't press charges. Yet in the back of his mind, he wasn't sure.

"She's supposed to work tonight. She's going to hurt. We found his license in a brown wallet. There was a few hundred left in it. The killer doesn't care to take the money. He lives on 17 Cleeve St. I'll go check out his place."

George left the scene. He looked up Harold in the phone book. He was married to a Cindy Baker. He drove to his house and parked in the driveway. There was a yellow van in front of him. It must be the wife's car. He lived in a large yellow house with green shutters. There were pretty crabapple trees in the yard and lots of hosta plants near the house. Everything was past season.

He knocked on the door. A woman with gray hair opened the door. She was wearing a pink gingham dress and black tights. She had brown eyes. She wore black rimmed glasses.

"Are you Cindy?"

"Yes. Who are you?" She wasn't sure and looked a little skeptical.

"I'm Officer George Trent. I hate to be the one to break the news to you but your husband, Harold has been murdered."

"Oh my god!" Cindy began to weep uncontrollably. She led George into a living room. He sat down in an orange lazy boy chair. Cindy sat on the green and blue plaid sofa. She grabbed a Kleenex from the box on the coffee table. There was a stack of crossword puzzles. Her curtains were orange to match the chair. Against a wall was a collection of china plates hanging from hooks. She had more plates and vases in a corner cabinet.

There were a few fishing magazines also on the coffee table. George figured that they were Harold's. "Did your husband like to fish?" She stopped sobbing for a quick moment.

"Yes. Sometimes he went fishing on Sundays with his friend, Tony."

"Where did your husband work?"

"He was a policeman in Kingston."

"I'm not sure if I knew him."

"He would have retired in ten years."

"How did your relationship go with him?"

"It's been rocky for the last six months."

"How so?"

"We've been sleeping in separate bedrooms. I think he had an affair on the side. Kara Willoughby. He was also playing tennis and I found out she played with him. I hired someone to follow him and the guy sent me pictures of them kissing in a nearby hotel. I couldn't look at him after that. I don't know if they ended the relationship. Where did you find him?"

"He was found naked in his car across from Tangoes."

"Jesus. Isn't that a strip club? Why would he be there?"

"Your husband paid for a prostitute last night. It cost him one thousand bucks."

"Bastard."

"Sounds like it. But nobody deserves to be killed. Someone waited for him. We're investigating right now."

"I hope you catch his killer."

"It's a serial killer. The person has killed three other johns. We haven't been able to trace anything yet."

"Is it a man or a woman?"

"It could be either." George said. "The person attacked a prostitute but didn't kill her. We're wondering why not?"

"She got lucky. I'm afraid I don't have anything else to help you out." George stood from the chair. "Again I'm really sorry to be the one to tell you. Good-bye." Cindy closed the door behind him.

George got in his car and turned on the ignition. After backing out of the driveway he headed over to the Auto body. He needed to talk to Jason. Once he got there he got out of the car and walked inside. There was a large man standing behind a red counter. He had frizzy orange hair and green eyes.

"I'm looking for Jason."

"That's me. What do you want?"

"I want to ask some questions about Bernie. We're guessing he didn't show up to work on Friday and Saturday. Did he have Thursday off?"

"Yes, he did. I've been trying to get a hold of him. He's always on time."

"We have reason to believe that he was killed Thursday morning. We discovered his body in the living room of his apartment."

"Holy toledo."

"You said it. Too bad for Bernie. Was he a good worker?"

"He sure was. He was very good at fixing cars. What happened to the poor guy? How was it done?"

"He was shot dead and strangled in his living room. Did he ever have any fights with anyone?"

"His ex-girlfriend, Ava came in a few months ago bitching him out. She was crazy. She really lit into him. We almost had to call the cops on her. She could have beat him up. Maybe she did it."

"Did you know he went to Tangoes and paid for a hooker named Sarah? There was also one named Susie. Did you know anything about that?"

"Sure. He told me about it. He had a tape of him and Sarah. There wasn't one of Susie. Wednesday, he told me Susie was a lesbian. I was shocked."

"Yeah. Susie told me that."

"Who found his body?"

"Sarah."

"Why was she there?"

"She got attacked by the killer and thought it was him."

"Bernie wasn't a killer. He was a sex maniac. I'll give him that. I hope you find his killer."

"Thanks for the information."

"No problem." Jason got back to looking at paperwork. George left and got back in his car Next he drove over to South Haven to visit Kara Willoughby. She lived on Chestnut Drive. He parked on the side of her street. A woman with short blond hair was cleaning her car. She was wearing a white shirt and blue jeans. She had deep blue eyes the color of the sea. She was beautiful. George could see why Harold fell for her. She was a little younger than Cindy. She had small breasts. She was wearing blue earrings the shape of circles. They were almost a teal color and had black markings on them. They looked like something Susan would wear. The girl was busy clipping her rose bushes. Deadheading seemed to be the thing to do this time of year. She looked up when she saw him coming.

"Hello, Kara?"

"Hi. Who are you?"

"I'm Officer George Trent. Harold Baker is dead. Where were you last night?"

"I went to my book club then came home. How did you know about me and Harold?"

"Cindy had you followed. Someone has murdered Harold last night. He went to Tangoes and paid for a hooker. We found him dead in his car across the street."

"Damn him. I tried to convince him to divorce Cindy. I didn't know that he paid for a hooker. What a chump. I wish he was still here so I could punch him." Kara said with

vehement anger behind her breath. "We had a tempestuous relationship. We had sex in the sauna room at the fitness club. His wife could never get pregnant. His marriage was deteriorating and I helped it along. We had great sex. We couldn't keep off each other."

"Did you know anything about Tangoes?"

"No way. Not a thing. What a dirty secret."

"There's usually things a man doesn't tell a woman."

"I guess that's one. Maybe I'll call Cindy. I could say I'm sorry."

"You could talk about things and get it out in the open."

"Yes. She probably hates me though."

"Can you think of anything out of the ordinary as to who might have done this to him?"

"I don't think that I can. Sorry, I can't help you." George thanked her and let her get back to trimming her gardens. George left.

George went to see Ava next. She lived in South Haven but wasn't answering her phone. He discovered that she worked for JC Penneys. He decided to find her at work. He walked inside and asked a clerk about Ava. She pointed him to the lingerie department. Once in the bra section of the store he saw a girl sorting underwear. She was busy hanging some on the fixtures. She was tall and skinny. She had long black hair that was down to her waist. She was wearing a blue head-band. She had on a blue shirt with a v-neck. She had on a black dressy skirt and blue pumps.

"Are you Ava Peabody?"

"Yes. What? Who are you? I don't know you."

"I'm Officer George Trent. Where were you on Thursday morning?"

"I was on my way to work. Why?"

"Bernie Blackmore has been murdered."

"Holy crap. Who do you think did it?"

"We're not sure. When is the last time that you saw him?"

"Last week. We broke up a few months ago. We had a nasty fight. I wanted more and he wanted out. He didn't want to be tied down. I wanted to get engaged but he didn't. I scared him away. We were together last year and he beat me up. He got arrested. Then we got back together. It was great for a while."

"Why did you go see him last week?"

"I lied and told him I was pregnant. I wanted him back."

"That's not good. You don't want to trap a man. Did you know Susie Lockhart or Sarah Fisher?"

"No. Was he going out with them?"

"They were hookers. He paid to have sex with them. Someone is killing the johns. Bernie wasn't the only one."

"So you're dealing with a serial killer."

"Did Bernie have enemies? Anyone he may have picked a fight with?"

"Not that I know of. Although last week he said that someone was following him. He asked if it was me."

"Was it?"

"No."

"Thank-you. If I have any more questions, I'll call you." George left the store. He went to several florist shops asking about any unusual large purchases of roses from men or women. Everyone told him there was nothing out of the ordinary. Just men buying roses for their wives or girlfriends. Normal stuff.

At lunchtime he arrived back at the station and found Susan. She had two Italians waiting for him. He picked one up and began to eat. It had extra pickles in it. He also loved the Macdonald's Mc Rib sandwich. He was sorry that they weren't selling it anymore. He loved their French fries. Maybe he would stop there tomorrow for lunch.

"Did you find out anything about the autopsies?"

"The time frame for Bernie's death is definitely Thursday morning. His rigor mortis was developing. It looks like the bullet killed him but not right away. That's why he was strangled too. There was ligature markings on him. And several bruises. We found no fingerprints or DNA. I took fingernail clippings to see if he fought the killer. Nothing. The killer is wearing gloves. That's why it's so hard to find anything. Harold died sometime last night around three am. Death by bullet wound. It's a 9mm gun with all the victims. We do have a breakthrough though. There were several black hairs found nearby Harold this morning. One was short and the other was longer. It's been analyzed and it's definitely real hair. It's not from a wig. And they weren't Harold's hair. Congratulations! Our killer has gotten a little sloppy. If only we were able to get a trace of DNA, you could nail the son of a gun. Thank me, babe." George gave her a nice juicy kiss on her cherry red lips. He snuggled next to her for a few minutes.

"This is great. It narrows it down. How long was the other hair?"

"Pretty long. It could be a woman's hair or a man with long hair. At least you can probably cross off some of your suspects. Good, huh."

"You bet your pretty behind."

"You want to see it later?"

"Do I get my private showing, honey?"

"You name the time, I'll be there. I've got that sexy red nightgown I could show off for you."

"I'm there. I better head out right now. I've got some more things to check up on. I've got several suspects with black hair." George kissed her again and left the room.

Sarah walked out of the hospital. Judy was there to drive her home. Later she would take a taxi to her car. "How did it happen? You look like crap."

"I got home and I was attacked in my mudroom. The person dropped black roses on me."

"Holy god. You're so lucky you didn't get killed. Do you think it was the man who stabbed that woman? He probably followed you home. Christ, Sarah. Maybe you need cops at your house." Sarah didn't want to tell her about the cops that were outside Judy's house. Sarah was still afraid something bad was going to happen to Judy. "Did you break anything?"

"No. I'm lucky. My ribs are just bruised." Judy dropped Sarah at home and headed back to work. Sarah fished out her license for her guns and called a taxi to take her to her car. Once she got to her car, she got in and drove to the police station. Larry was in his office. She walked in and slammed the proof of license on his desk. "Here, you prick. Can I have my guns back?" Larry looked at the license for a minute. He looked at Sarah.

"How do I know you didn't forge this? Watch your mouth, you bitch." Larry got up and went into another room for a minute. He came in holding her guns. He stepped really close to her and aimed the guns at her crotch. "You breathe a word about pressing charges and I'll come hurt you myself. Does the hooker understand?" He was pressing hard and it hurt.

"Move the gun from my crotch, you jerk. I could tell

George about you." His other hand came up and squeezed her face. She felt like spitting in his face. She didn't like Larry anymore. Finally he handed her the guns and her license. She wanted to aim a gun at him. She could say it was in self-defense.

"Be careful with those."

"They're for my protection, prick. Come near me again and I'll shoot you." Sarah walked away. She had had enough of Larry. She couldn't believe he had just threatened her. Would he really hurt her?

She drove away and went to the mall. She wanted some new clothing. She bought three black dresses, another pair of stilettos and a black bra and see through black underwear. She went into another shop and bought some new luggage. Maybe she was entitled to another trip somewhere exotic. Maybe China. Once back home she went online and purchased a new Dell computer to replace a broken one. She wanted to be able to type up her poetry and email her friends. She also liked to shop on E-bay. Sarah had a small collection of porcelain dolls. She liked the Dianna Effner dolls. She really wanted to email her friends.

Later, Ava headed home from work. She was glad that Bernie was dead. He deserved it. She really wished that she had his baby though. She didn't tell the cop that she knew all about Sarah and Susie. She knew about Tangoes. She was jealous that Bernie went there. She was really jealous of Sarah and Susie. It wasn't fair that he was having sex with them. He should have been having sex with Ava. She was pissed. She had gone to his house. She discovered the tape of Bernie and Sarah. She was in a rage. That was why she went to see him at work last week. She was really angry. She followed him everywhere he went. The jealousy was burning into a heated rage. She missed having sex with him. She felt that if she couldn't have sex with him, nobody could. Life wasn't fair. She had wanted them to get married and buy a house together. She wanted his babies. She had been screaming bloody murder. She slashed her pillows with a knife one night she was so angry. She wanted him to be alone and miserable pining for her. She wanted him to miss her and want her back. She didn't care if he beat her up again. She would let it slide because she loved him so much. She had gone to Sarah's house. She waited in her car. She wanted to punch her lights out. She wished that she was dead. She had hated seeing the tape.

She drove home and the rage was killing her. Life wasn't fair. She didn't want Sarah to live. She arrived at her house and stepped inside. She went to her kitchen. Her kitchen walls were a soft peach color. Her counters were yellow. She opened a cupboard and pulled out a Ramen Pride macaroni noodle dinner, filled it with water and tossed it into the microwave. She looked at her sharp knives. She thought of Sarah and Susie. She was jealous of Susie too. They had bigger breasts than she did. She thought of the strippers. She wondered if that

was something she could do. Would she be able to sell her body? She wasn't very good at dancing. She pulled out her meal and sat down and the oak table to eat it. She had a white doily resting in the middle and there was a basket full of bananas.

Later in the evening Sarah got in her car and drove to Tangoes. It was Saturday night. The club was packed. Sarah was wearing a glittery black dress. It looked like a flapper girl dress. Her black stilettos matched. Benny was at the bar serving beers to customers. Sarah went into the dressing room. She sat in the brown chair and combed her hair. She grabbed her blush and mascara out of her purse and applied it to her cheeks and eyelashes. She was wearing a purple antique necklace tonight. It was very expensive. She liked a Victorian catalog called Victorian Papers. She shopped on it a lot. There were also dolls in it that she bought for Beth.

A few minutes later Susie came in. She hugged her gently. "Does it hurt? The police officer told me that you were attacked by the killer. You were very lucky." Susie put her hands on Sarah's shoulders and massaged her neck for a few minutes. Sarah closed her eyes and tried to relax. It was working. Susie had the magic touch. Susie looked at Sarah and wanted to kiss her but she didn't. She was with Betty now. It wouldn't be right. But Susie remembered Sarah's body. That night with Johnston had brought up memories. Susie had wondered if she could go back in time. She couldn't. She felt happy with Betty. She didn't want to wreck things. Susie dropped her hands and left the room.

Sarah looked in the mirror and thought back to that night with Susie. It was about four months ago. They had both gotten drunk at a different bar. Susie had slipped her some drugs and Sarah was feeling no pain. They were with some young guys for a while. Sarah told one of them that she was a stripper. The guy had grinned and began fondling her. She had worn a pretty brown dress that was clingy. She had on her black stilettos. Later in the evening Sarah and Susie drove home to Sarah's house. Once they got inside, they started laughing. The drugs were still in high gear. Susie followed Sarah to her bedroom. Once the door was shut, Susie approached Sarah and pulled off her dress. Sarah was wearing a pink bra and matching underwear. Susie was wearing a magenta dress. Sarah undid her buttons and revealed Susie's black bra. Susie continued to slip out of her dress. The two began kissing each other passionately on the lips and caressing each other's breasts. Susie nudged Sarah near the bed and pulled off her underwear. Then Susie began licking her vagina. After a little while they bumped cunts and kissed fiercely. Sarah had never been with a woman before and was curious to know what it felt like. Besides, she was so drunk and was half aware of what she was doing. It was a one night stand and never happened again.

Sarah came back to the present moment at hand. She waited. There was no Benny. He didn't come in to rape her tonight. She wondered why he didn't. Maybe he was too busy. Maybe Susie told him what had happened.

Sarah walked up on the stage. She began to sing and dance. Susie was also on the stage dancing. There was a third girl, Rebecca that was also dancing. She had black hair and cornflower blue eyes. A fourth girl, Louisa was also dancing. The stage was loaded tonight. After a short bit all the girls stripped off their dresses. Sarah was wearing thigh highs and her red licorice underwear. Rebecca had on white lace thigh highs and nothing else. Susie was wearing a black corset that revealed her large breasts. She had on nothing else. She was wearing red stilettos. They danced around each other and took turns dancing around the pole. Sarah danced near Susie. Susie grabbed Sarah's waist and pulled her to her. They bumped cunts for a few minutes and Susie licked Sarah's tits. It was all an act.

Sarah danced her way into the audience and let the men place money in her g-string. Susie stuffed her money in her corset. Men's hands felt Susie's breasts as they slowly stuffed the money into her corset. Susie straddled a young guy with blond hair. His hands grabbed her ass.

Sarah was still hurting from the attack. She wished she was at home resting. She did a lap dance for an older man. Slowly his hands stuffed a ten dollar bill into her g-string. He licked his tongue and placed his hands on her breasts. He looked like a grandfather.

Later she saw the man with the black ponytail sitting in the back. She went over to him and danced erotically for him. She wondered if he was going to pay for her again tonight. "Are you going to give me some cream for my coffee?" he asked with a smile on his face.

"It will cost you, sugar daddy." She rubbed her body all over him and he gave her some tips.

Later the four girls began dancing on the stage again. Louisa danced by herself. The other three began dancing close to each other and began fondling each other. Sarah

licked Rebecca's tits. Rebecca looked at her. It was the first time Sarah had ever done that to Rebecca. Rebecca smiled and massaged Sarah's breasts. Several men in the audience smiled and whistled.

The man with the ponytail drank his beer. He was wearing a red shirt tonight and black dress pants. He kept watching Sarah. He thought of the video he had taken. It was evidence.

Later Sarah went back to the dressing room and counted her tips. Some of it would pay for her necklace. Benny came in and pocketed some of the money. She watched him leave. When he was gone she pulled out fifty dollars that he didn't see. She stiffed him some of his money. She had been doing it for about five months. So far he didn't know about it. She put her dress back on and left the room. She went upstairs to room number six. Rebecca, Susie and Louisa were in other rooms. They were busy. She opened the door and walked in. She placed her purse on the table and looked at the person in the room.

It was the stranger with the camera. Sarah thought the stranger was a little creepy but there was going to be money for her after she was done. "Hey, babe. Come here." She was reluctant but she slowly shimmied out of her dress and left it on the floor. She walked over to the stranger and let the person slide hands up her thighs. The stranger pushed her down on the bed and began eating her red licorice underwear and putting a tongue into her vagina. The stranger undid clothing and pressed bodies with hers. For about an hour the two fucked each other hard. Finally the stranger grabbed the camera and began snapping pictures. The stranger took about fifteen to twenty pictures and Sarah posed for the stranger.

Finally the stranger got dressed and gave Sarah six hundred dollars. She pocketed one hundred and left the

room. Benny was in the office counting his money that the other girls had given him. He got Sarah's money too. He was looking at eight hundred dollars for doing nothing. He liked being a pimp.

Sarah went back upstairs to room seven. The man with the ponytail was waiting for her. "Come sit down beside me, sugar."

Sarah sat next to him. His red shirt was unbuttoned and revealed a hairy chest. His hands wrapped around her waist. "Careful of my ribs."

"Why? What happened?"

"I was attacked at my house last night. My ribs hurt. Luckily nothing was broken."

"I'll be careful. I'll be gentle tonight." The man grabbed her and pulled her to him. He began kissing her shoulders and collarbone. Then his lips grazed her neck. His hands pulled at her dress. She took it off quickly. He undressed to his paisley boxers. He caressed her breasts and gently sucked on them. He penetrated her and had sex with her. He was sweet and full of desire. Sarah liked it. She wondered why he didn't want her sucking on his dick tonight.

Suddenly he kissed her lips and began to kiss her fervently. His desire mounted. She wasn't sure what to think. The johns usually didn't kiss her on the lips. She felt his hands getting tangled in her hair. Then he touched every inch of her body. He kept kissing her lips gently and passionately. He kissed her tenderly on the cheeks and shoulders. He found her breasts and caressed them and then rubbed her abdomen. His tongue grazed her body with lovely desire. Then their lips met while He penetrated her vagina again. He was gentle and romantic. It was different and Sarah liked it. She wanted more of this. It felt new.

The man got dressed and Sarah followed suit. "Would you like to know what my name is?"

"Okay." Sarah looked at him. She didn't want him to go.

"It's Douglass Harrington." He kissed her lips again slowly. "I didn't hurt you did I?"

"No. It was nice."

"I like you, Sarah. Please stop stripping. You can find something else." He handed her six hundred. She put it in her purse. "Can I call you? What is your home phone number?" Sarah smiled. She grabbed a piece of paper and wrote down her name and number for him. "What are you doing Sunday night?"

"I've got the night off."

"How about I come over to your house with a pizza? What do you like on it?"

"That sounds great. I like mushrooms and pepperoni."

"Sounds good. I'll call you tomorrow and get directions. How about eight pm?"

"Sounds good." Douglass kissed her good-bye and left the room. Sarah smiled. There was something about him that she liked. Could it be the beginning of something fresh? He was the second person that asked her to stop stripping. Sarah walked down the stairs and went into Benny's office. She handed him two hundred. She felt guilty about pocketing the extra hundred but she smiled to herself as she left the room. Benny deserved to be stiffed. She didn't like Benny raping her. It was wrong. He needed to get his just desserts. Too bad for Benny. As it was he was making a killing off all of the girls. Five or six nights a week Benny got eight hundred dollars at least and all for doing nothing. Sarah wondered what he did with his money. He must be saving it. He lived in a cheap apartment and usually dressed down. He didn't wear expensive clothing. Maybe he was investing his money in stocks or savings bonds. He probably had enough money to retire early. Sarah wondered why he didn't travel or see the world. He had enough money to do it if he wanted to. Once Benny had told Sarah that she was special. She wondered what he meant by that. She

wasn't sure about Benny's private life. She often wondered if h e had a girlfriend. He didn't quite look like the type to settle down. He was too rough around the edges. He was always wearing tee shirts with vulgar language on them.

She left the bar and walked two blocks to her car. The night air was really cold and frigid. At least there was no snow on the ground yet. She got to her car and fished out her keys. She saw the pistol in her purse. Her other guns were back in their hiding places at home but she liked to carry her pistol with her. She felt safe with it. She didn't want the killer attacking her again. She turned on the ignition and began the drive home. Suddenly she thought of the killer. What if the stranger went after Douglass? Would he be in danger? She began to cry. The wet tears rolled down her cheeks like a speed train. She wiped them away with the palm of her hand. She didn't want anything to happen to Douglass. What if the stranger with the camera got killed? Was there going to be another john murdered? Sarah hated that everyone connected to her was getting killed. She wondered what she could do to stop it. Yet she was no detective. She wasn't very good at finding clues. Her name wasn't Nancy Drew. She used to like to read her books when she was a little girl. She liked to watch Wonder Woman and Father Murphy. She loved Little House on the Prairie. Laura Ingalls Wilder was her favorite childhood heroine.

She got home, unlocked the door and went upstairs to bed. She slipped on her lace nightgown and drifted off to slumber. She dreamed of Douglass. She dreamed of making love to him again. She had a date tomorrow. He wasn't going to have to pay her. Suddenly she sat up in bed. What if he was the killer? Was he going to work his way into her life and kill her? She didn't know anything about Douglass. Maybe he had a violent past. She wondered if he was the one sending her black roses. She wondered if she did the right thing by saying yes to him. She shrugged her thoughts aside. He had to be okay. She wanted to believe in good things. She wanted her life to change. She was really letting his words sink in. She thought of George. She just had to make the plunge.

Do something different. Something lovely and brand new. A new life. Sarah smiled to herself. She really wanted it. She was changing her heart around. Then she started thinking about all her bills and she put a frown on her face. It wasn't that easy. And there was Benny. What would he do if she told him of her plans? She fell back asleep.

Beth was sleeping in her bedroom. It was painted purple. Her mom had painted it last year. She had a white dresser bureau across from her bed. There was a little mermaid lamp on it and a stack of her clothing that needed to be put away.

Her bedspread was a pretty patchwork comforter. She had a pink flannel blanket. She was sleeping soundly. She had her favorite Web kinz pony next to her. She was dreaming of pug dogs. She was excited to get a new puppy. She had decided to name it Patches. Her red hair was in two ponytails. She was wearing flannel pajamas with polka dots. A bunch of her stuffed animals were in a corner.

Suddenly the door opened slightly. Beth slept through it. She was completely unaware of anything. She felt something on her lips and quickly woke up. She couldn't speak. She had a big piece of duct tape across her mouth. A rough hand pushed down on her. "You scream and I'll kill you, kid."

Beth now was frightened. She peed her pants. She looked up at the stranger that held her tight. The stranger was wearing a mask and a black trench coat. The stranger grabbed her and picked her up. She kicked but the stranger was too strong. The stranger brought her past the living room and carried her outside. The stranger got to the black Porsche and opened the trunk. The stranger tossed her inside and shut the door. She was trapped. The stranger got in the driver's seat and drove away. The stranger had some bait. The stranger liked little kids. The person wasn't planning on killing Beth. The stranger wanted to keep her as a trophy. The stranger just wanted to get Sarah all worked up. This was going to do it. The stranger smiled. The stranger reached over to the tray between the seats and grabbed a handful of dry roasted peanuts. The stranger looked at the gun on the seat. The stranger needed to kill someone. The stranger wanted the cops to know that the stranger wasn't done.

The stranger wanted to show off the artwork. The stranger thought of Beth. The stranger had a room picked out for her. The stranger hoped that she would like it. She was going to stay there for a while. She was going to be a new guest. The stranger liked company.

Susie slept next to Betty. It was two am. Suddenly Betty woke up and started kissing Susie. They kissed each other on the lips. The kiss turned into sweet desire. Susie tangled her hands in Betty's curly blond hair. Susie thought Betty was beautiful. She had completely forgotten about Sarah. She remembered back and smiled. They had had some fun. It had been worthwhile. But Susie had wanted more and Sarah wasn't ready to give it to her. Sarah had just been experimenting.

Betty lowered her lips to Susie's breasts. Betty's tongue slowly circled her breasts and sucked fervently on her tits. Susie moaned and massaged Betty's breasts. Betty kissed every single inch of Susie's abdomen. Betty quickly began to eat Susie's cream. Susie climaxed and screamed "I love you, Betty." Betty came back up and pressed her body against Susie. They rubbed their vaginas together and made love. At three am they fell asleep and dreamed of all the sweet tomorrows. They were madly in love with each other. Betty wanted to marry Susie. They had talked about adopting a child. They liked the thought of raising a little baby or a toddler. They had been to the adoption agency together.

The stranger entered the green ranch house. The rooms were dark and there was no sliver of moonlight to cast into the house. It was a dark and dreary evening. The sky was purplish black and there were no stars to be found. The stranger went into the kitchen and grabbed a knife. The kitchen counter was filled with ceramic cows. There was an empty cup of coffee left out on the counter. The white sugar bowl was filled with organic sugar. There were red roses on the table. They were in a pretty purple vase.

The stranger walked into the living room. There was a yellow couch. On the coffee table there was a Sarah Lee coffee cake that was half eaten. The dirty plates were still on the table. There were a lot of chick flick movies on a shelf next to the television. The curtains were of yellow lace. The blinds were closed. There was a black cat resting in the corner. A white kitten was curled up next to the other cat.

The stranger walked past the bathroom and opened the door to the bedroom. The stranger walked over to the bed. The two women were sleeping peacefully together. The woman with blond hair had her arms wrapped around the other woman's naked breasts.

The stranger was jealous. The stranger felt a powerful surge of rage. The stranger had felt the urge to be in the middle. The stranger had wanted to be on stage in the middle of the three women fondling each other. Orgy. The stranger had never experienced an orgy before. Suddenly the stranger's wrath was winning. The stranger quickly slit Susie's throat. She opened her blue eyes in complete surprise. She tried to utter something. She couldn't make out who the person was. The room was too dark and her eyes hadn't adjusted. After a few minutes she was dead. There would be no more Betty for her to hold. No more drugs to snort. Betty was sleeping soundly. The killer scrawled sinner on Susie's body and threw a black rose on the bed nearby. The

stranger had also left a black rose on little Beth's bed. The stranger left the house and got in the car. The stranger drove home. The stranger parked the car in the driveway. The stranger opened up the trunk and grabbed Beth. She was shivering and her pants were wet. The stranger brought her inside. The stranger opened the door to the basement. The stranger brought her to a metal door. There was a little cot and a bucket in the middle of the room. The stranger set her down on the cot. "Be a good girl. If you're bad, I'll kill you. That's a promise." The stranger tossed her Web kinz on the cot with her and left the room. It wasn't the best accommodations but it would work. The stranger hoped that she would like it. The stranger liked Beth. The stranger liked having a child. The stranger had always wanted one. Now the stranger had one.

Beth wished that she was sleeping in her bed. She wanted to be in her own home. She cried for her mom. She wanted Judy. Mommy would come for her. Mommy wouldn't forget about her. Aunt Sarah would look for her too. She lied down on the cot. It wasn't very comfortable. The walls were made of solid stone. She wanted so badly to cry for help. Maybe someone would hear her. But then the stranger would come down and kill her. She had to stay quiet. She saw a dead person on the movie Friday the 13th once. Mommy didn't know that she had seen parts of that movie. Daddy had let her watch it. She missed Daddy too. She liked it when Daddy let her do things that Mommy wouldn't let her do. She really liked the junk food. She was happy that Mommy and Daddy were getting back together. She wished she was home.

Sarah woke up the next morning. It was Sunday. She heard the geese honking as they flew by in the deep blue sky. The sun's rays shined through her window casting light into the room. She looked at her white vanity table. She had a few silk flowers in a blue vase. The vase had been her mother's. Some of her jewelry was also passed down from her mother. She also had some of her grandmother's things. She missed them. Her grandmother had died of old age. Yet Sarah still missed being around her. She had been really funny.

She got up and undressed. She stepped into the warmth of the shower. The warm water pulsed gently against her body. She lathered herself with her rose soap. She rinsed off and turned off the water. She toweled off with her purple towel. She walked into the bedroom. She opened her drawer and fished out a floral bra and put on frilly yellow underwear. Then she pulled on a cashmere sweater that was pink. She slipped into a pair of blue jeans. Then she put on her fuzzy pink slippers.

She went downstairs and started her coffee machine. She sat at her kitchen table and had a bowl of apple jacks. She went outside and retrieved her morning newspaper. She sat on her living room sofa and read the news. She liked the Home and Family section. She usually cut out the recipes. She liked to see who was getting married. She hadn't seen Justin's name. She could have missed it. She was sure he was probably married now. Sarah wanted to be married. She had to change her ways. Maybe Douglass would be the guy for her.

Julie got up and put on a plaid shirt and a pair of blue jeans. She combed her hair and went downstairs to the kitchen. She poured herself some cocoa puffs. While she ate she thought back to her childhood. That had been a long time ago. She thought of her brother. Then she thought of her mother. She felt fierce daggers that turned into anger. She hadn't liked what her mother did to them. She felt really embarrassed. The feelings came back to her in a flash of lightning. She remembered. She had partly liked it. Julie was wondering if she would end up like her mother. Sometimes the pattern continued its cycle. Her sister had gotten lucky.

Julie had dreamed of the woman again. She really wanted her. Julie also really wanted a child. She had dreamed of little girls. She wanted one of her own really bad.

Judy woke up and went downstairs. She turned on the television. It was on Nickelodeon. It was eight am. Beth would be up at any time now.

Judy was in her flannel nightgown. She opened her refrigerator and grabbed a Dannon blueberry yogurt. She reached for one of her mother's spoons. Sarah had gotten their grandmother's set. She brought it into the living room and wolfed it down. Soon it was eight thirty. Still no Beth. She was sleeping late this morning. She should be excited. They were going to go pick out a pug dog this morning.

Judy read a chapter from her James Patterson book. She was reading Sail. It was really good. Judy had read quite a lot of his books. Her favorite was Along Came a Spider. By nine am she had read through several chapters and there was still no sign of Beth. It wasn't like her to sleep so late. Usually Beth woke up at seven am.

Judy went upstairs to Beth's room. She walked inside and discovered the empty room. She was shocked. Where was Beth? Judy opened up her closet. Just her sleeping bag was in there along with clothing and dolls and games that she didn't play with anymore. She had put Beth to bed at eight pm last night. Suddenly she saw the awful black rose on the pillowcase. Judy was horrified. Someone had come in and taken her little girl. Judy put her hands to her head and let out a bloodcurdling scream. She ran out of the room. "Beth! Beth! Beth!" She only received harrowing silence. How she wished that her daughter would answer back. She wished that Beth was playing a game of Hide and Seek. She wanted this horrid nightmare to disappear. Judy checked every room but turned up nothing. She ran out into the yard but found no shred of evidence pointing to where she could have gone to. Beth was long gone. Judy wondered where she was. She hoped that she was safe.

Judy called Sarah. She picked up on the third ring.

"Sarah! Beth is missing! Oh my god! She's gone. My baby is missing. Someone has taken my child."

"Jesus. Call the police. I'll be right over."

"Someone left a black rose on her bed. It's the same person that attacked you. Why Beth?"

Sarah felt her heart stop and then the subtle pounding echoed. The killer had Beth. Sarah hung up the phone, grabbed her keys and got in her car. She; drove really fast past the speed limit. In ten minutes she arrived at Judy's house. She hugged her sister. Judy had been crying. She had a pink Kleenex box on the coffee table.

"The cops will be her in a few minutes. I'm so worried about Beth. What if she's hurt? There was no ransom note. The person doesn't want my money. Sarah what if my baby is dead?" Judy began crying uncontrollably. Sarah held her and consoled her.

Beth was gone. There was no little girl here to draw pictures. No little redhead to talk about school. There was an absence of silly laughter.

There was a knock on the door. Judy opened the door and let the police officers into the living room. Larry saw Sarah. "Judy's your sister?"

"Yes." Judy looked at Sarah.

"He knows you? Oh, that's right. The woman who was stabbed. I forgot."

"A stabbed woman? " Larry looked skeptical. "It wasn't anything like that. Your sister lied to you."

"What? There was no stabbing?" She looked at Sarah. She had a guilty look on her face.

"Please explain. If there was no stabbing, then what actually happened?"

"Your sister is a prostitute and a stripper." Larry said. He enjoyed getting Sarah in trouble.

"What the hell? Sarah, my god. Don't tell me that it's true. For Christ's sake."

"I'm sorry Judy. I'm not like you. I'm not a play by the rules kind of girl. I never have been. You just didn't see it."

"Why the hell do you do it?"

"I've got lots of bills to pay. I enjoy it."

"What? Selling your body? Mom would roll over in her grave. Please stop! There's other ways to pay your bills. Prostitution is dangerous. "

"It's not that easy. I make good money. Sometimes I get eight hundred bucks in one night. Good money, Judy."

"But it's what you're doing. It's like a crime. Sarah. You could get a disease."

"Come on Judy. Drop it. I don't want to discuss it anymore."

"Hey," George said. "Let's talk about your missing child. Isn't that more important. You and Sarah can argue another time. Maybe Judy will smarten you up. Lord knows that you need some change in your life. We're planning on shutting down Tangoes anyway. It's an underground club and some of the things that are going on are illegal. So when did you last see your little girl?"

"I put her to bed at eight pm. I stayed up until ten pm doing some laundry. I was behind and needed to get caught up. After that I went to bed. I didn't hear anything unusual. I got up this morning at eight am. She didn't come down so at nine am I went up to her bedroom and found her gone. There was a black rose resting on her bed."

"I hate to tell you, but there's a killer that is leaving black roses at the crime scene. It's probably the same person. I'm just preparing you for the worst."

"The killer is trying to torment me. Now the person has Beth and knows that I'm going to be really upset. What can

you do to find the killer? Before Beth is dead." Sarah cried. Sobs were mounting in her throat.

"We can put out an APB for Beth. We're searching for a person with black hair. We'll look everywhere that we can. We can have the news station advertise for help. Maybe someone has seen her. All I can say is I hope we find her. Hopefully she doesn't turn up dead like everyone else. I'm very sorry this has happened to you." Said George. Judy grabbed her blue wallet and pulled out Beth's school picture.

"I hope this helps you. She was wearing pink flannel pajamas. Her pony Web kinz is also missing."

"Can we have an article of her clothing? It will help the search dogs sniff for her scent."

"Okay." Judy stood up and went upstairs. When she came down she handed George some polka dot underwear and some white socks.

"Thank-you, Judy." He placed them into a baggie. "So we can honestly say that maybe she's been missing since ten pm last night. Larry saw that your back door was left open ajar. That's probably how the stranger got in. We'll be on our way so we can start the search. If we don't find a dead body perhaps there will be a sliver of hope. That's all that we can pray for." George and Larry left the house and drove away. Judy and Sarah sat in the living room and cried with each other.

Betty woke up. The black clock said nine thirty am. She reached over and caressed Susie's breast. It felt sticky to the touch. She kissed her tit. Susie was very still. She peered over at Susie and stared in horror at the blood on her neck. It had made a pool of blood on her chest and the white satin sheets were bloody. Betty sat up and screamed. She couldn't stop. "Susie! Susie! Oh shit." She quickly jumped off the bed. She looked again and saw the word sinner on her chest. Betty picked up her cell phone and called the cops. "Help! My girlfriend has been murdered. Oh, please help!"

"Are you safe?" asked Lucy.

"I think so. I don't know. I think I'm alone. I haven't checked yet. I just woke up a few minutes ago and saw her dead. My girlfriend is gone!"

"I'll send someone right over." Lucy hung up the phone and called George and Larry. Betty began to cry. The last thing she wanted was for Susie to be dead. She looked at Susie again and saw the black rose on her body. It was ominous.

Betty put on a cream colored shirt and a blue skirt. She didn't want to be found naked when the police arrived.

She walked into the living room and sat on the pink couch. She carried a box of Kleenex with her. She didn't see any sign of an intruder. She felt relieved. She wondered why the killer hadn't killed her too. She thought about their lovemaking last night. She would have told her that she loved her had she known that it would be the last time. She had wanted to marry Susie. They would soon hear from the adoption agency. Betty cried again. She really missed Susie. Why did the killer want Susie dead? Was it because she was a stripper. Or did the killer not like lesbians?

Ten minutes later there was a knock on her door. Betty opened the door and greeted Larry and George. She brought them in and showed them the bedroom. Larry walked in

and started taking photographs with the Polaroid. "When did you discover she was dead?" George asked.

"I woke up at nine thirty am. I looked over and saw her like this. I might have fallen asleep by three thirty or four am. I think the killer must have come in while we were sleeping."

George called the forensics team. He saw a closer look at Susie and felt like throwing up. The killer had used a different weapon. There was no gun this time. George looked at the picture on the wall. It was a reproduction of The Scream by Edvard Munch. On the nightstand there was a glass crystal container. He opened it up and found an antique red ruby necklace and some matching earrings. There was five hundred dollars left out on the nightstand. It seemed that the killer didn't care about money. So far at all the murders there was no trace of a weapon. On another wall there was a picture of pink peonies. On another bureau there was a container of Georgio talc powder. A half used bottle of Loves Baby Soft perfume was next to it. There were seven or eight lipstick containers on the dresser.

The forensics team came and started dusting for fingerprints, taking photographs and searching for DNA samples. He took another look at Susie. He felt bad for Betty. She obviously was very upset. It must be really hard to lose a lover. George would be really devastated if something happened to Susan. He saw the word sinner again. He wondered how old the killer was. Did the killer have a family? Or did the killer capture Beth so that the killer could have a family? He hoped that she wasn't being harmed. George hoped that he would find her alive.

"I've found a footprint," said one of the men from the forensics team. There was a footprint in the middle of a pool of blood on the floor. George took a picture of it and planned on showing it to Susan. Maybe there would be another break

in the case. George came across a framed picture of Susie. It was when she was a little girl. She had been really cute. The photo was a black and white picture of a little girl with ponytails. Why had Susie turned to stripping? What was her reason? George wanted to nail Benny. He wondered if Benny had anything to do with the murders.

George watched one of the guys place Susie in a body bag. That seemed so final. Susie would soon be sent to the funeral home for an autopsy. Susan would be busy for a while. Susie had another dead man at the home. He had died of a heart attack. There was no need for an autopsy on him.

George walked into the living room and found Larry investigating. "I've been in the kitchen. One of their knives is missing from the butcher block. Maybe it is the weapon of choice."

"They found a footprint. The killer is getting messy. Let's get going. I need to send this picture to Susan and I've got to get Beth's picture to the Channel 3 news station. Maybe they can air it this evening. We've got to start searching for her." George and Larry left. Betty was still sitting on the couch and her eyes were red from crying. She now faced a life without Susie.

The stranger sat in the red chair while painting more roses black. Some of the paint dripped onto a paper towel. The stranger sat near pictures of Sarah. The stranger had a picture of Susie dead and bloodied. The pictures of Sarah were quite revealing. They were black and white. The stranger had a fascination for photography. The stranger's black mug of hot chocolate rested on the coffee table. It was getting cold. The stranger's gun and knife were also on the table.

The stranger looked at the L.L. Bean boots. There was a little blood on one shoe. The stranger had been careless and given them another clue.

On another table there was a picture of Sarah when she was younger. The stranger had stolen it and put it in a blue frame. There was another picture next to it. It was a photograph of a little girl. Her name was Lindsey. She had been the stranger's first victim. The stranger kidnapped her seven years ago. She had brown hair and blue eyes. She had been wearing a yellow dress and had been playing in a nearby park. The stranger had told her there was ice cream in the stranger's car. She had believed the stranger and followed to the car. Once there the stranger had forced duct tape on her and tossed her in the trunk. The stranger had kept her in a cape house in South Haven for a few days. She screamed too much so the stranger killed her by strangulation. The stranger buried her body in some nearby woods. The police never found her body.

Several years later the stranger began capturing women. The stranger would bring them to the house, duct tape their mouths and tie them to the guest bed. The stranger's brother was the only other guest. The brother knew about all the women. The brother came over and raped the women and left. The stranger wasn't sure if the brother knew about the deaths. There were about twenty women in all. The stranger

strangled them and buried them in the woods. To this day the women are still missing.

The stranger looked at a childhood photograph. It hadn't been a happy childhood. The stranger and the brother had been molested and abused by their mother. Their father died not knowing.

The stranger remembered Beth. It was ten am. She hadn't been fed yet. The stranger got up from the chair and walked into the peach pantry. The stranger grabbed a box of cocoa puffs and brought it into the kitchen. The stranger poured some into a blue bowl and poured in some milk. The stranger grabbed a spoon and poured some orange juice into a Blues Clues cup. The stranger had purchased the cup for Lindsey. The stranger walked into the basement and opened the metal door to Beth's room. The stranger set the food on the floor. Beth was lying on the cot. The stranger went over and touched her curls. The stranger wanted to sit down and comb her pretty hair later. "Eat a good breakfast and I'll be good to you. Scream and you die. Just like little Lindsey." The stranger left the room and let her eat in privacy.

and left the room. Beth felt dirty. She cried. Her mom had told her not to let anyone touch her private parts.

The stranger sat down in the chair again. The stranger hadn't felt a little girl since Lindsey. The stranger liked innocent children. It was a whole new world for them. The stranger thought back to childhood days. The stranger remembered the mother coming into the room and touching private parts. The stranger got used to it. Beth would get used to it too. The stranger really liked Beth. The stranger didn't want to kill her. The stranger wanted to keep her forever. Maybe the stranger could bring Sarah over and they could take care of Beth together. The stranger grabbed the car keys and headed to work.

At eight pm Sarah opened her door for Douglass. He was standing on her doorstep with a bouquet of pink roses. She was glad that they weren't black. His hair was in a ponytail and he was wearing a blue shirt and blue jeans. On his feet were Adidas sneakers. He took them off at the door. He had on blue socks.

"Hello. Thank-you for the flowers. They're really nice." Douglass followed her into the kitchen while she reached for a green vase. She filled it with water and placed the roses in it. Douglass set the pizza on the table. They ate the pizza. After they went into the living room and sat down.

"So what do you do, Douglass? You know what I do."

"I'm a reporter."

"Oh. Am I in trouble?"

"Of course not. Why do you do what you do?"

"I like the money. I have lots of credit cards to pay."

"How many men have you had sex with?"

"Why do you want to know?"

"I'm just curious. How many?"

"A lot."

"Do you like Benny?"

"He's alright. He fucks me. I don't like it. I wish I didn't have to give him some of my money. He doesn't know that I pocket some of the money."

"Does he rape you? He could get in trouble. Have you thought about pressing charges?"

"He's my pimp. He'd get his thugs to beat me up."

"What is his last name?"

"Jacobs. He lives near Tangoes. Why?"

"Just like to know about people. Is he married?"

"No. He never had kids."

"Does he have any family?"

"I don't know. He never talks much about his private life."

Sarah said. *"I don't want to talk about Benny. Do you have any sisters or brothers?"*

"I have a brother."

"Is he older or younger?"

"He's older. He lives in South Haven."

"What about your mother and father?"

"They're dead. My mother died when we were in high school. She got drunk and drove her car in a lake near Kingston. She couldn't get out in time and she drowned. I was in the tenth grade when it happened."

"That must have been awful. What about your father?"

"He died of lung cancer. That was a few years ago. What about your parents?"

"They died in a car crash three years ago. Some drunk driver hit them. They died instantly. I live in their house."

"When did you start stripping?"

"Four years ago. I had a lot of credit cards to pay."

"So you're a shopaholic?"

"You could say that. I bought a lot of expensive stuff. I met Benny four years ago."

Douglass saw the leather journal on the table. *"What is that?"*

"That's my poetry journal. I write in it during the day. I also like to plant flowers in my garden. I've got lots of rose bushes. I like to read Harlequin romances. How about you? What are your hobbies?"

"I like to play golf and watch baseball."

"My sister's daughter, Beth has been kidnapped. There's a killer on the loose. The stranger is putting black roses on all the victim's bodies. I've been getting threat letters and black roses in my mailbox and on my car. There was a black rose in Beth's room. The killer has her."

"Wow. I'm sorry to hear that. What are the police doing?"

"They put out an APB for her and they have been searching for her all day. Beth's picture was on the news tonight."

"Do you think the killer is someone you know?"

"I'm not sure."

"The killer didn't kill you. What do you think the killer wants?"

"I think the killer wants to torture me. The stranger had a chance to kill me and didn't jump on it. I just hope the killer spares Beth. She's my only niece."

"What about old boyfriends?"

"I had one ten years ago but he's not a killer. He couldn't have. I had an abortion. That was hard to go through."

"The killer must go to the club. The killer must follow the johns and kill them. The killer likes to write sinner on their bodies. The killer has a thing against sinners. I found out your friend, Susie was murdered. I've been following the crimes. The cops have been giving me information for my stories."

"Susie was murdered? Oh my god!" Sarah put her hands to her face and gasped. "Oh no!"

"Did you have a relationship with her?"

"Why? Did you see us touching each other on stage?"

"Yes. I was curious."

"She came to my house once. We had sex. We were also really drunk. I wanted to know what it was like. I'm really not a lesbian, but I experimented once. It never happened again. Then she met Betty and started dating her."

"Did you like having sex with her?"

"It was fun and different."

"The killer knifed her. The killer was using a gun and suddenly switched to a knife. What about the other strippers?"

"Rebecca Simpson. The fourth one is Louisa."

"Is Rebecca a lesbian too?"

"No."

"She caressed your tits."

"But she's not a lesbian."

"She could be a closet lesbian. Maybe she is and you don't know it. Maybe she liked Susie too. There could have been some jealousy going on."

"You think she could be a killer? You think she could have killed out of jealousy?"

"Maybe she's in love with you and doesn't want to kill you. But maybe she had a relationship with Susie too and was jealous when Susie started dating Betty. Relationships are complicated. What does Betty do?"

"Betty works at the cinema. Susie's brother introduced them to each other."

Suddenly Douglass stopped talking and asking questions. Instead he reached over and held her face. He began to kiss her softly and slowly. He wanted to linger and taste her essence. She kissed him back. She wasn't used to kissing on the lips. Suddenly his kisses became urgent and passionate. They locked eyes and deepened their passion. It smoldered like hot flames. He kissed her cheeks her forehead and lowered his mouth to her neck. His lips softly grazed her collarbone. She wound her hands through his hair. He leaned her back against a pillow and kissed her with deep desire. He didn't care how many men she had slept with. He found it hot that a woman had known her intimately. She sent fervent hot tempestuous kisses to him. He was fast with his hands and slid them underneath her pink sweater. She quickly undid the buttons on his shirt one by one. His tan hairy chest was revealed. She wound her hair through his hair. He leaned her back against a pillow and kissed her with deep desire. He didn't care how many men she had fucked. He found it hot that a woman had known her intimately. She sent fervent hot kisses to him. She pulled off her sweater and revealed her pink bra. She was wearing feminine dainty stuff today. He lowered himself to her and began kissing her chest. His teeth raked her nipples. His hands fumbled with the clasp

"How much."

"Twenty thousand."

"Wow. What did you buy?"

"Lots of stuff. I went on vacations. I've been to Barbados, Cayman Islands, Europe, Sweden, Italy, Rome, Ireland, Hawaii and Greece."

"Holy crap, you get around. When did you have time to do that?"

"After I broke up with my boyfriend ten years ago. I travelled. Then I've had to pay it all back."

Douglass kissed her lips tenderly and lay next to her warm body. "Was the abortion hard for you?" He watched to see her reaction.

"It was. I had wanted the baby. He gave me $1,000 to get rid of it. It was like killing a living being. Afterwards I cried for a while. I eventually healed and got over it."

Douglass looked at Sarah. "You could find a decent job to pay your bills back. Being a stripper isn't a way to live. If you ask me, that club needs to be shut down and then none of you will be stripping."

"It's not that easy, Douglass. If I leave Benny might send his thugs to beat me up. Louisa tried to leave once and she was nearly beaten to death. She lived but she was afraid to stop stripping. Benny Is like the mafia."

"If you leave I could protect you." Douglass wanted to protect Sarah. He was beginning to really like her. At first he had played along with the prostitution game. Having sex with her and that other john had been interesting, but not really his cup of tea. But he had played along with it. He was glad that he had taped it. He wanted evidence to get the club closed down. He and George were in on it together. The cops wanted the club closed. They just needed enough hard evidence to do so. It would happen sooner or later.

"I don't want to get you in danger." Douglass quieted Sarah

with more delicious showered kisses. Eventually they fell asleep in each other's arms. Sarah dreamed of Douglass and a new life. She dreamed of other jobs. She dreamed of being an actress. It was something she had dreamed of when she was a child. She had either wanted to be an actress or a doctor. Yet she didn't really want to cut anyone open. The thought of blood was disgusting. When she was a teenager she knew she wasn't cut out to be a doctor. Her sister used to want to be a country singer. Both girls had beautiful voices. They had several video tapes that their mother had produced of them doing marathon singing. They used to pretend that they were producing a radio show. The girls were always close when they were growing up. They had wonderful parents. Their luck had run out when their parents died. Sarah still missed them immensely. Sarah also dreamed of yellow roses. She loved that color. If she was to repaint her kitchen someday she decided on yellow. It was bright and lively. Change was a good thing. She decided that she would be ready for it soon. It was just a matter of time. She could get through it.

The stranger drove home from work. The stranger parked the car in the driveway. The stranger stepped out and grabbed a paper bag filled with groceries. The stranger had made a stop there on the way back.

Once inside the stranger turned on the lights and brought the bag into the kitchen. The stranger pulled out a box of Spongebob Squarepants macaroni. The stranger got a pot of water and put it on the stove. While the water boiled the stranger pulled out the rest of the groceries. The stranger had bought honey buns, ring dings, applesauce, a box of Cheerios, honey, a jar of jam for muffins and a case of beer. The stranger pulled out a bottle of Budweiser and drank it. When the macaroni was al dente the stranger drained the water, added the cheese and put some macaroni in a blue bowl. The stranger got a Blues Clues spoon and poured a glass of milk. There were several reminders of Lindsey. The stranger missed her. The stranger hadn't wanted to kill her. But Lindsey had proved to be a bad naughty child. It had to be done.

The stranger opened the basement door and went downstairs. The stranger opened the metal door. Beth was sleeping. The stranger went over and woke her up. She sat up and became nervous. The stranger set her food down on the floor. The stranger went over and sat next to Beth. She held onto her Web kinz pony. The stranger slipped warm hands under her pajama top and massaged her boobies for a little while. "Give me a big smile. Women like their boobies rubbed. Doesn't it feel good?" The stranger stuck hands into her pants and massaged her private parts. She began to squirm. "Don't move or I'll kill you." She sat very still while the stranger probed her vagina. "Touch me." The stranger ordered. Beth touched the stranger's private parts. She didn't like it. She felt like throwing up. Suddenly she upchucked. "You bad girl. I didn't tell you to do that! Just for that I'm not going to give you your macaroni."

The stranger got up and retrieved her bowl of macaroni. The stranger left the room and locked the door.

Beth began to cry. She wiped away her warm wet tears and began to sob some more. She didn't like the way the stranger touched her. It was dirty and uncalled for. Now her pajamas were caked in throw up. She felt sick. She at least decided to drink the milk. She was thirsty. After she went back to dreaming about her Mommy rescuing her. Mommy had to be trying to find out where she was, She couldn't stay here forever. She wanted to get to see her friend Lucinda again. Beth liked school. She was a social butterfly.

The stranger went upstairs and sat down in the orange chair. The stranger devoured the macaroni. It tasted good. The stranger began to paint more of the black roses. The stranger wanted to send some more to Sarah tomorrow. The stranger thought of little Beth. The stranger didn't want her to throw up again. If she did the stranger might have to kill her. Later the stranger went to bed. The stranger didn't feel like killing anyone tonight. The stranger dreamed of sweet bloody bodies. The stranger dreamed of Sarah. The stranger was almost ready to bring her home. The stranger wanted her blood. It was almost time.

Sarah woke up on Monday morning. She looked over and saw Douglass sleeping next to her. She couldn't believe that he had stayed the whole night. She wondered if she deserved him. It had been a long time since she had had a boyfriend. She was a prostitute. She didn't deserve a nice guy. She sucked men's dicks for a living. Why would this man care for her? Their passion had been wonderful. She wondered if it could last. She wanted it to.

Could he be a killer? What if he was trying to charm his way into her life. Maybe he would kill her when she leas

expected it. He was still a stranger. She didn't know him very well.

She knew that she loved having sex with him. It felt different with him. It was more like making love. She really liked it and wanted more of the sweet desire. She wanted to care deeply for Douglass.

Could she really stop stripping? She owed so much money. She wished that she didn't have to give Benny so much of her money. She enjoyed stiffing him. He didn't know.

Douglass woke up and began showering her with sweet soft kisses. She really hoped that he wasn't the killer. She cast her dark fears aside. She tried to stop thinking of black roses. She didn't want to see any more of them. They made sweet erotic love again. The glorious sun shined through her curtains and cast patterns upon the carpet. It was going to be a lovely day. "I'm going to look for puppies later. Would you like to come with me?"

"It sounds great, but I need to go to work."

Douglass got up and started getting dressed. Sarah watched him.

"What are you doing tomorrow afternoon?" Douglass asked.

"Nothing so far."

"Would you like to see a movie? Black Swan is playing."

"Sure."

"I'll pick you up at twelve thirty and we'll see a matinee." He kissed her good-bye and left the house.

Douglass left Sarah's house. He really liked her. The moment he saw her in the club he liked her. Maybe Sarah wouldn't like him if she knew what he really did for a living. She might get angry. He was really a private detective. He was investigating the underground strip club. He wanted to nail Benny. He had begun to go to the bar and pretended to be part of the crowd. Benny was running the underground strip club.

The men really weren't supposed to touch the women. Douglass was privately working with George and Larry. They all wanted to shut down the club. Douglass had at first wanted to get close to Sarah to find out information. But his desire for her evolved. He wanted her. Now that he knew about Sarah's friend Louisa getting beat up he was determined to talk with her. Maybe he could get some of the girls to testify against Benny. It seemed as though he was raping Sarah and beating up Louisa. They could charge him with assault. He could go to jail. It seemed as if the girls were covering up for Benny. They were afraid of him. That's why he wanted Sarah to know he could protect her. She had to know that she would be safe. He carried a gun and wasn't afraid to use it. He wanted to let Sarah know that she wouldn't be in trouble. He wasn't out to nail the prostitutes. He just wanted Benny behind bars. He wondered if Benny had something to do with the murders. Maybe Benny and Rebecca were working together. Food for thought.

He thought of what had happened last night. It was so sweet and he desperately craved more of her lovely taste. He could feel his desire mounting as he thought about her. He hoped that she would seriously consider what he asked her to do. Could a stripper stop stripping? He wanted her to change for him.

Then George told him about the murders. He started doing more investigation work. So far there had been five murders. The four johns and the lesbian stripper. After what Sarah told him about all the black roses, he was convinced it all had to do with Sarah. Then Sarah told him the killer had her niece. Douglass had to find out who the killer was. Maybe he could work with George and Larry to save the niece. Hopefully she was still alive.

He had tracked other unsolved cases. He had researched missing women in the area. Over the years there had been about twenty cases of unsolved missing women. He was baffled and

wondered what had happened to them. He wondered if they could be related to the new murders.

Douglass called George. "Hello?"

"Hi. It's Douglass. Is there anything new with the murders?"

"There was a footprint found in Susie's bedroom. We found out it was from an L.L. Bean boot. So far we're looking for a man or woman with black hair. You have any leads?"

"I talked to Sarah some last night. I asked her about Rebecca. I'm also wondering if it could be her. I'd like to find out if she's a lesbian. She could have killed Susie because she chose Betty over her. She's got black hair."

"She wears stilettos."

"Maybe she also has L.L. Bean boots."

"Possibly. Explore all the angles. I've interviewed several people with black hair. I might go back and question them again. One of the girls is Julie. She works at Dunkin Donuts. She got dumped by Johnston. She has the jealousy motive too. She has black hair. There's also Ava Peabody. She was Bernie's ex-girlfriend. Again the jealousy motive comes into play. Again black hair. Both are still suspects in my book. Can't rule them out. Maybe either one of them went over the edge."

"I'm wondering if all those missing women could be related."

"I don't know. You think the killer used to bury the bodies and now is deciding to show us the work? Why would Rebecca want to kill all those women?"

"Maybe she had sex with them and then disposed of the bodies. We're definitely dealing with a serial killer. Could you have someone run a background check on Benny Jacobs. I'd like to know more about him before I nail him. Sarah said that he sent thugs to beat up Louisa. Maybe we could get the girls to testify against Benny."

"I'll look into it." Douglass hung up the phone. He didn't

tell George that he had been intimate with Sarah last night. He was attracted to her. He wanted more of her. Was it going to turn into something other than lust? He was ready for a relationship. Sarah was the woman for him. He was determined to make her turn into a good girl. He knew that it could be done. He had a goal.

Sarah got out of bed. She slipped into a pair of pink underwear and a satin bra. Then she dug into her drawers for a peach pullover sweater and a pair of pink sweatpants. She pulled on some ivory socks with brown polka dots on them. She went downstairs and slipped on a pair of shoes. She grabbed her keys, left the house and stepped into her car. She drove to see the puppies. Once she got there she saw the whole litter. She picked out a little girl puppy. The dog breeder said she could pick it up in a few weeks. It wasn't ready to leave the mother yet.

Sarah drove to visit Judy. She stayed with her for a while. They called the cops to see how the search was going. There was nothing new. No trace of Beth anywhere. Judy's eyes were red rimmed from crying. She really missed her little girl and was afraid that Beth was dead. She didn't want her gone from this earth. Later Judy left for work. She needed to keep herself occupied.

Douglass called Sarah. "Hi, honey. I found out a new clue about the killer."

"What is it?" Sarah was curious.

"The killer wears L.L. Bean boots."

"Wow. Are you getting closer to solving it?" Sarah really hoped they would find the killer.

"I think so. I want to let you know something. I wasn't completely honest with you about what I do. I'm really a private detective and am keeping tabs on Benny. I don't want to get you in trouble. I'm sorry. I want to let you know that I wasn't using you. I really like you and want to see more of you."

"I like you too. Are you working with Officer Trent?"

"Yes. We're trying to catch the killer. I have reason to believe that Rebecca is the killer. She's got that jealousy motive. Especially if she is gay. Can you do me a favor and try to get closer to her so we can find out if it is her?"

"I'll try. I'll be seeing her this evening. Are we still on for tomorrow? I heard that Black Swan is really good. Natalie Portman plays a ballerina."

"Cool. I heard that it is a creepy movie."

"I like those kinds of movies. I'll see you tomorrow. I really enjoyed last evening."

"Me too." Douglass hung up the phone.

Later in the evening Sarah got in her car to go to Tangoes. She had changed into a little black dress and red stilettos. She got there and went into the dressing room. Sarah saw Rebecca sitting down. Rebecca was combing her hair. She was wearing a red dress. "Hi, Sarah."

"Hi, Rebecca. Can I ask you something personal?" She sat down next to Rebecca.

"Sure, anything for you, Sarah." Rebecca turned towards Sarah and put her comb down. She locked eyes with Sarah.

"Are you a lesbian? I'm sorry. Maybe that's too personal." Rebecca studied Sarah for a minute.

"Yes I am. I thought you would never ask." Rebecca moved closer to Sarah and began to kiss her lush lips. Sarah kissed her back. At first the kisses were soft but then Rebecca became more passionate. Her hands held onto Sarah's waist. Then she got up and straddled Sarah. Sarah started to slide her hands up Rebecca's dress. She felt Rebecca's pussy. She wasn't wearing any underwear. "I love you, Sarah. I've always loved you."

Rebecca pulled at Sarah's dress and began kissing her breasts. Her teeth raked Sarah's tits and her tongue glided ever so slowly around her perky round breasts. "Susie and I broke up because I told her I wanted you." Sarah felt Rebecca rub her vagina. Sarah began fervently kissing her lips again. As she kissed Rebecca she wondered if Rebecca could really be the killer. She had promised Douglass she would get closer to Rebecca to find out. "It's almost time to go on stage. I've got to see a john afterwards. Can I come to your house after?"

"I've got to see a john too. My place sounds great. We can get to know each other better. I'm glad you want to see me too. I love you. I've loved you for a long time." Rebecca kissed her again and left the room. Sarah didn't really want to know Rebecca intimately but she had promised Douglass She would try to find out. She had to know if Rebecca was the killer. She

could be onto something. She didn't realize that Rebecca was in love with her. Why did Rebecca kill all those johns?

A few minutes later Benny came in. He grabbed Sarah and threw her against the floor. He quickly unzipped his jeans and lowered his body to her. He thrust his rock hard dick into her vagina and banged her hard. His rough hands pushed up her dress and tore at her edible underwear. Afterwards he pulled out and squeezed her face really hard. "You better not stiff me of my money anymore, you bitch. Louisa told me that you were stiffing me. Benny slapped her in the face a bunch of times and punched her stomach. He stood up and kicked her several times. "Get up, you whore. Make me some money, you lousy bitch." He slapped her again and left the room. Before he left he said, "You stiff me again and I'll have you beaten up like Louisa was. I'm the all powerful. You had better listen to me."

"I might stop stripping for you, you jerk! You're raping me. I might press charges."

Benny came back and kicked her in the ribs. "I might have you killed." He left. Sarah was afraid. She didn't want to die. Would Benny really kill her? Was there more to Benny than just the pimp? Sarah was angry with Louisa for tattling on her. She wondered why Louisa did that.

Sarah slowly got up and went out on stage. She began to dance erotically. As she danced her thoughts were about leaving the stage. She wanted out. She was angry with Benny for raping her. She had just about had enough. Rebecca danced next to her. She played up to Rebecca and danced for her. She had to be a really good actress and let Rebecca think that she loved her back. Sarah would pretend that she was also a lesbian. She wanted to get to the bottom of the deaths. Douglass had been right about Rebecca all along. She wondered if George knew. Rebecca stripped down to a red corset. It revealed her rather large breasts and was attached to nylon stockings. The men could see her vagina.

Louisa was dancing and sliding down a pole. Sarah felt like clawing her. Sarah would have kept quiet if it was Louisa stiffing money from Benny. Louisa had a son to support. She was lucky that Benny hadn't gone after her little boy. Louisa had long red hair that was curly and thick. She was wearing a black bra and black thigh highs. She was tall and slender.

A little later Sarah saw Douglass in the audience. She didn't know that Douglass was planning on paying for Louisa tonight. He wanted to convince her to testify against Benny. He had to get all his ducks lined in a row.

Sarah stepped out into the audience and did a lap dance for an older man with blond hair. He was wearing a White snake tee-shirt and blue jeans. She rubbed her body all over him. His hands held her butt cheeks and his head pressed into her breasts. He gave her some good tips and then she went over to several other men.

She and Rebecca did a lap dance for a younger man. They rubbed their bodies all over him and gave him sweet erotic kisses. Then they turned to each other and danced together for a few minutes. Rebecca was so close to Sarah she could smell her breath on her.

Then Sarah went to a man with brown hair and did a lap dance for him. He caressed her thighs and gave her some more tips. As Sarah danced she thought to herself that this may be her last night to strip and be a prostitute. Then she was going to walk off the stage and never come back. She was determined to do it. Now she had Douglass to protect her. Could he keep Benny away from her? She hoped that he would. She had Douglass and George on her side. She couldn't quite count on Larry. He had wanted her behind bars. There was something about him that wasn't quite right. Maybe he was keeping secrets from George. He seemed like a dirty cop.

Later Sarah was back in the dressing room counting her money. Benny came in and took what was his. Rebecca came

in and started massaging Sarah's neck. Her hands slipped into Sarah's dress and rubbed her breasts. "I'll see you later, my love." Rebecca kissed her long and hard on the lips. Sarah thought that later she would be the perfect little actress for Rebecca. She had to play into her mind and get Rebecca to trust her. She had to find out.

Sarah went upstairs to see the last john. This one was seriously going to be her last. She would never do it again. She would have to find a normal decent job. Something new was calling her name. She went into the room and fucked the brains out of the last john. She got five hundred bucks. When she was done she ran past the office. She wasn't planning on giving any of it to Benny. Let him come beat her up. She would have Douglass to back her up. She wanted him more than anything. She wanted to be his forever. She wanted a whole new world to open up for her. The meeting with Rebecca would be her last. She would be the professional actress. She wanted to act. It was her dream.

Douglass waited in room seven for Louisa. She came in and sat down. She was expecting him to ask her to take her clothing off. She was wearing a brown dress with sequins on it. It flattered her curly red hair fell around her oval face. "Can I ask you some questions?"

"Okay. You don't want to have sex?"

"No. I'm a private detective. Sarah told me that Benny hired some thugs to beat you up. When was that?"

"Last year. I tried to stop stripping."

"I may be able to bust Benny. Did he let you know that it was him?"

"Yes. He told me if I stopped being a stripper he'd kill me. I was afraid. I was in the hospital for more than several days. I thought they were going to kill me."

"Did Benny ever rape you?"

"No. Just Sarah."

"What do you know about Benny?"

"He has a deck of tarot cards. He said he would decide my fate."

"Do you have any kids?"

"Yes. I have a little boy. He's with a babysitter right now."

"What is his name?"

"Luke."

"After Luke Skywalker? What do you know about Rebecca?"

"She's gay. She likes to go hiking and fishes sometimes. She's been hunting. She wanted me to go hunting with her once. I didn't go. Her being gay made me uncomfortable. I'm not that way. If that suits her that is fine with me. I prefer men. I'm dating someone right now."

"Does he know you're a stripper?"

"No."

"Could I ask you to testify against Benny? If I get you and

*Sarah to testify, he could go to jail. He's done some bad things.
Rape and beating you up are two of them. You could change
your life around."*

*"I'm not sure. He'd probably kill me. I've got a kid to think
about. I'm all he has. His father lives in another state and isn't
part of our lives."*

*"I could give you protection. I'm working with the cops. We
could have someone watch your house at night until everything
is over. Benny needs to be in jail. Help me nail him."*

*"Alright. I've been wanting something new. I'd like to be
a waitress."*

*"That's a good job. Lots of tips and you don't have to
take your clothing off to get them." Douglass said. "Here's my
card. Call me if you change your mind. Douglass gave her five
hundred for her time. He knew that Benny was waiting to
collect. The bastard. Douglass said good-bye to Louisa and left
the room.*

Sarah drove to Rebecca's house. She stepped out of the car and knocked on the purple door. The cape house was white with purple shutters. Rebecca opened it and let her in. Sarah walked in and set down her purse on Rebecca's green chair. Rebecca was wearing nothing. Immediately she moved in on Sarah and pulled off her dress. She tossed in on the floor. Quickly Rebecca pressed her body against Sarah. Rebecca picked her up and carried her to her red kitchen. She leaned Sarah against her island. Sarah's back was pushed against the gray granite countertop. A purple bowl filled with delicious cherries fell to the floor with a thud. A blue vase with black roses tipped over. Sarah wrapped her long legs around Rebecca. They became romantically entangled. Rebecca wrapped her arms around Sarah. She kissed her with sweet swollen desire. Sarah could taste the hint on white zinfandel on Rebecca's lips. Rebecca and Sarah rubbed bodies for a little bit. Rebecca opened her refrigerator and pulled out a jar of hot fudge and a spray can of whipped cream. She pressed Sarah against the floor smack in the middle of the fallen cherries. She sprayed the cream and poured the fudge on Sarah's breasts and vagina. Rebecca fervently licked her all over. She sucked Sarah's tits and raked them gently with her teeth. Then she ate the fudge and cream off her vagina. She licked Sarah's clitoris and probed deep, deep and deeper into her vagina. Sarah moaned. "Harder!"

Rebecca's hands massaged Sarah's breasts while she ate her cream. Sarah had an orgasm.

"I love you, Sarah."

They rolled over onto each other and caressed passionately. They ate some of the cherries.

An hour later after several rounds of sex and lovemaking and fucking Sarah against a wall they fell asleep. Sarah woke up at three am. She looked over at Rebecca. She was fast asleep. This was Sarah's time to do a little investigating. Sarah stepped out of the bed and started looking around. She opened up

Rebecca's closet. Rebecca had lots of dresses, There were also a bunch of cashmere sweaters. On the floor were a bunch of stilettos. There was a pair of L.L. Bean boots. She picked them up. They were a size eight. Later she would tell Douglass that Rebecca had the same shoes as the killer. She saw no sign of black roses in the bedroom. On a shelf there were a bunch of thigh highs. They were mostly black and red. There was a vibrator next to the thigh highs.

Sarah slowly opened drawers of Rebecca's bureau. There was mostly clothing and socks. Rebecca liked wool socks. In one drawer she found a wad of cash. There were several thousand. She put it back and closed the drawer. She wondered what Rebecca was going to spend that on.

Rebecca had some Britney Spears perfume on her dresser. There was also some Elizabeth Taylor perfume. She had a woven basket filled with hair accessories. Rebecca liked head bands. By the bureau on her blue carpet there was a pair of brown furry slip on shoes. They looked comfortable. Sarah grabbed the Britney Spears perfume and sprayed her neck and wrists. Sarah was wearing a pearl bracelet that had been her mother's. She also wore her cameo necklace.

Sarah liked Rebecca's vanity table. She saw a bouquet of yellow roses on it. She wondered if Rebecca was going to paint them black. What if Rebecca was really the killer? Sarah had to find out where Beth was.

Sarah left the bedroom. She went to the living room and slipped her dress back on. Rebecca had a blue sofa and a white wicker coffee table. There were red roses on it. There was a jar of black paint next to them. Sarah was horrified to see the paint. Had she just had sex with the killer?

Then Sarah saw a box of photos on the table. She sat down and looked through them. There was a picture of Rebecca and Benny. Rebecca also had several pictures of the stranger that Sarah had fucked. Sarah wondered why Rebecca had

these pictures. There was a picture of Benny when he was younger. There were several pictures of Rebecca's parents. There was another picture of a younger Benny with the stranger. They looked like friends. Sarah wondered how they knew the stranger. Sarah confiscated some of the pictures and put them into her purse. Sarah opened a nearby drawer and found a 9mm gun. She didn't know that Rebecca had access to a gun. Sarah became sick on thinking of Rebecca killing all those people. She searched for Beth. Sarah was frantic to find her. She had to be here somewhere.

Sarah turned around and saw Rebecca standing in the doorway to the living room. She was wearing a red housecoat. She moved to Sarah and tried to kiss her. Sarah pushed her away.

"Have you been sending me black roses? What are you doing with black paint?" Sarah backed away from Rebecca. She was suddenly afraid of her. She wondered if it was Rebecca's plan to kill her. But Rebecca said that she loved her. She wouldn't kill someone she loved. Would she?

"I sent you some of them. I wasn't the only one. I love you."

"Why black roses? That's creepy."

"I only wanted to scare you a little bit. I'm sorry."

"Why do you have all those pictures of Benny? Who is that stranger?"

"Benny is my cousin. The stranger is also my cousin."

"Your cousin?"

"Yes."

"When you say you weren't the only one sending me roses. Who else is sending them? I demand to know. Where is Beth? Do you know where she is?"

"I can't tell you. I promised not to tell."

"Beth is hanging by a thread. Have you killed the johns? Answer me Rebecca."

"No. I haven't killed anyone. Come back to bed. I want to have molten lava sex again."

"I can't. I'm sorry, Rebecca. I only had sex with you to find out if you were a killer. I can't see you anymore."

"I thought you felt the same way about me! You used me! You bitch!"

"I've got to go. Have a nice life. I'm done being a prostitute."

"Benny is going to come after you." Sarah ran out the door with her purse and got in her car. She quickly drove out of the driveway and headed home. She pulled out her phone and called Douglass.

"Hello?" he said groggily.

"Douglass. It's Sarah. Sorry to wake you. Rebecca is a lesbian but she isn't the killer. She was one of the people sending me black roses. She had some black roses and paint on her coffee table. She confessed to doing it. She said someone else is also sending them to me. She wasn't the only one. She's in on something. Maybe she's covering up for the killer. Get this. She's related to Benny. Her last name is Simpson. She is his cousin. She is also a cousin to the stranger that I had sex with. Maybe they're in on it."

"Wow. Maybe Benny is the killer. I was suspecting him too. Maybe we can put him away for a long time."

"Rebecca has a 9mm gun. I found it tonight. She could have been lying to me. She did say that she wasn't the killer. Maybe she isn't."

"Was the stranger a man or a woman?"

"It was a man. He had black hair. Do you think it could be him? He definitely had the creep factor going for him. He had a camera and took lots of pictures of me. Maybe he was the person who sent me the pictures of the dead men."

"Could have been. Please be careful, Sarah. I don't want anything to happen to you. I just met you."

"The thought of having sex with him makes me sick. What if it is him? What if he or Benny has Beth? She could be dead by now. I'm afraid for her."

"I'm having George do a background check on Benny. I'll let you go and give him a buzz. I'll see what he came up with. I already miss you. I'll see you tomorrow. Are we still on for the movies?"

"Yes. Guess what?"

"What?" Douglass asked with curiosity brimming in his mind. "Is it good news?"

"I've stopped stripping. Tonight was my last night. I'm not going back. I had sex with Rebecca tonight to find out if she was the killer. I hope I've pointed us in the right direction. I'm sorry that I had to do that. But it seemed like the only way to get her to trust me. I won't do it again."

"I understand. You had to do what you had to do."

"She did own a pair of L.L. Bean boots. Do you think she could have been lying?"

"I don't know. It sounds like she is protecting someone. You should be careful of her. It's a little creepy that she was sending you black roses. Why would she do that?"

"I don't know. Well, I'm almost home. I'll let you go." Sarah hung up the phone. She stepped out of her car and went inside. It was four am. She left her purse in the car. The evidence remained inside her purse. Once inside she went upstairs and slipped on a long black nightgown. It seemed to match the black roses that she didn't see on her dresser. She fell asleep.

"Hey, It's me." Rebecca said. She was on the phone with someone. "She knows that I sent her some of the roses. What do you want me to do?"

"Stay there for right now. I'm going to go get her. It's time."

"Okay. Your secret is safe with me. I won't tell anyone."

"I know you won't."

"Are you going to kill her right away? Let me see her first. I've got unfinished business." Rebecca hung up the phone. The killer was on the way to get Sarah.

The stranger got in his black Porsche and drove to Sarah's house. He thought of Rebecca. He had to decide what to do with her. She knew too much. The stranger couldn't afford to let her open her big mouth to anyone. The stranger thought of little Beth. He had to decide what to do with her. He wanted to keep her to himself. For how long could he do it? That was the all telling question. The stranger watched the barren trees. Fall time was almost at it's peak. Winter was approaching rapidly. It was already becoming rather cold and frigid. The stranger wondered if he could keep Sarah and Beth long enough for Thanksgiving. He hoped that they would come around and love him. He loved Sarah so much. His heart was already aching for beating her up. He really didn't mean to do it. He had really enjoyed killing those other people. They were all sinners. Deep down he knew that Sarah was a sinner too. His feelings were so deep for her. He felt that he could forgive her. He had to let her know that she didn't need to be afraid of him. If she was not going to be able to do that then he ultimately was going to have to kill her. Slow and painful. He was sometimes ruthless.

A little while later Sarah woke up. She felt strong hands force a white cloth to her face. It was chloroform. Immediately she was knocked out. She didn't know what happened to her. She felt herself trying to resist deep sleep, but it was doomed to happen. She was going to miss her date with Douglass.

The stranger carried Sarah in his arms. She was limp and dangling in her black nightgown. The stranger walked to his trunk and opened it. He tossed her inside and shut the door. Then he got into the driver seat and drove to his home. Once he was there he opened up the trunk and carried Sarah inside to the guest bedroom. He tied her to the bed and left the room.

A little while later Sarah came to. She was a little groggy. She looked at her surroundings. She wasn't safe in her bedroom. She was in a small room with white walls. She looked at her wrists and discovered that she was tied to a bedpost. A red rope held her wrists and legs tightly. The killer had undressed her and put duct tape to her mouth. She tried to scream but her voice was muffled. She struggled to free herself from the bondage but it was useless. She was trapped in this hellish room. She didn't know where she was or what time it was. The room was still dark so she was guessing it was still early morning. She wondered if she was anywhere near Beth. She listened for her voice but heard absolutely nothing. All she got was dead silence. It was foreboding.

She began to cry. What if he had already killed Beth and she was next? She didn't want to die. She didn't want to think of Beth being in heaven. It was unthinkable. Sarah was cold and she needed to use a bathroom.

Ten minutes later the door opened. Sarah looked at the person in the doorway. She was completely shocked. It was Benny. What was he doing here? Was she in his home? Was Benny the killer? At first she thought maybe she could get him to help her. Maybe she could convince him to let her go. She needed to see Douglass. What would he think when he didn't find her at home? How many days would it be before Judy discovered her missing?

Benny was wearing a tee shirt that said Fuck You. He had on blue jeans and a red belt. He was wearing L.L .Bean boots. He undid his jeans and took off his shoes. Then he pulled off his plaid boxers. Benny straddled Sarah and penetrated her hard. He pushed and shoved. He took his belt and whipped her body with it. She cried out in pain. He was more severe than he had ever been. He pushed deeper and harder. He slapped her face several times. "You fucking bitch. You filthy whore." Benny beat her as if she were a rag doll. She wanted him to stop. She was

sorry for stiffing him. She wished he wouldlet her go. She wished he would take the duct tape off so she could talk to him. She had trusted him. She wondered when he would kill her.

Benny finally pulled out. He got up and put on his clothing. He lit a cigarette and puffed smoke. He walked over to Sarah and pressed the cigarette against her tit for a few minutes. Sarah winced. She tried to talk through her duct tape but he didn't listen to her. She tried to get free. She wanted to kick him. He deserved it. She thought if she was able to get out of this mess she would press charges against him. She wanted to see him rot in jail for what he did. He slapped her face a few more times and left the room.

Ava was resting on her blue sofa. She was watching Sleeping with the Enemy. It had Julia Roberts in it. She was one of Ava's favorite actresses. Ava was wearing a baby blue sweater and a brown woolen skirt. She was wearing black sweater tights. She had a pink blanket wrapped around her eyes were red rimmed from crying. She had been thinking of Bernie. Her moments of wishing he was dead were silently tormenting her. She really didn't mean to have those awful thoughts. It was really terrible that he was dead. She had wished that she could have him back. Now that was never going to happen.

She had come back from going to his funeral. It had been a sad event and there wasn't a dry eye in the place. She had placed a dozen yellow roses at his gravesite and she cried all the way home to her house. She had requested the day off from work.

She picked up a pink mug filled with hot chocolate. It was the kind with the mini marshmallows. A crystalline tear fell into it and evaporated into nothing. Another one rolled down her hot cheeks. She grabbed a Kleenex and blew her nose. She cried some more. She had wanted Bernie's children. She sobbed and thought about her bleak future. What would life be like without Bernie in it? She had been away from him for a little while but now her options with him were history. He would never pine over her. All she had now was his spirit.

She thought about someone new. Could she fall in love again? She didn't know. What pray tell awaited in her destiny? She didn't want to think about it right now. All she wanted to do was wallow in her dreary misery.

She had to get herself out of this funk. She had to dry her eyes and go to work tomorrow. That was her life right now. Maybe someday a man of her dreams would rescue her. She needed it. She threw out her slashed pillows. She didn't know why she did that.

Douglass arrived at Sarah's house at twelve thirty. He knocked on her door. Then he noticed that it was left open a little bit. He walked in and called her name. He received no answer. Sensing danger he pulled out his 9mm gun. He went into the living room and the kitchen. There was no sign of her in there. He went upstairs to her bedroom. He was shocked to see one dozen black roses on her bed. There was a note next to it. Douglass picked it up and read it. It said, "Come and get me you pig!" The killer had Sarah. He tucked the note into his pocket and fled from the room. He went outside and opened up her car. Her purse was still there. He fished out the pictures that Sarah had stolen from Rebecca. He saw the pictures of Rebecca, Benny and the stranger.

Douglass quickly got into his brown Sedan and drove to the police station. He got out of the car and ran into the station. He caught Lucy at her desk. "Where is George?"

"He's in his office." She watched Douglass run down to the office. He found George sitting at his desk eating a Hot Pocket.

"The killer has Sarah. I found this note on her bed along with a bunch of black roses. He's abducted her. She's in danger."

"Oh my god. That means if we find Sarah we'll probably find her niece."

"Sarah called me around three thirty this morning. She was driving home from Rebecca's house. She found these pictures." He dropped them on the desk and George flipped through them. "She had sex with Rebecca last night. She said that Rebecca sent her some of the black roses but there was someone else sending them too. Rebecca didn't tell her who it was. Sarah said that Rebecca is a cousin to Benny and this stranger. Sarah had sex with the stranger."

"Shit. I did the background check on Benny. Turns out he went to South Haven High School. He has a brother, Rory

Jacobs. The mother died about ten years ago. The father died while they were in high school. There was an incident at the high school. Both boys were brought to the nurses office. She found bruises on their bodies and suspected that either the mother or the father abused them. So they probably had an unhappy childhood. The brother works at The Photoshop in South Haven. Benny used to be a bouncer in a bar in Kingston. Then five years ago he opened the underground strip club."

"I met with a prostitute named Louisa last night. I'm getting her to testify against Benny. He hired thugs to beat her up. She was in the hospital for several days. This was about a year ago. She had tried to stop stripping. Benny has also raped Sarah. We can send him to jail."

"Wow. So we have enough to nail him. What should be our next move?"

"I have this gut feeling that Rory is the killer. Do you want to come with me on a stake out?"

"Sure. Let me call Susan to let her know where we are going. I'll call Larry too. We may need back up." George grabbed his coat and followed Douglass out to the Sedan. It would be more discreet than the squad car. George called Susan and Larry. They were on their way to 17 Baxter Street in South Haven. Once they arrived they parked across the street from the blue cape house and waited for some action. While they waited they ate some donuts and drank coffee.

A little while later a yellow Ferrari parked in the driveway of Rory's house. They watched as Rebecca got out of the car. She was wearing a blue sweater and blue jeans. She wore red stilettos. She walked into the house and disappeared.

Sarah waited. She needed to pee really bad. The room was lighter now as the sunlight cast a pattern from the yellow curtains. Suddenly the door opened. Sarah looked at the person in the doorway. It was Rebecca. She went over and straightened some of the black roses. "I'm sorry, Sarah. It had to be this way. They told me to let them know when you were heading home. I had to let them know."

Sarah tried to talk through the duct tape. If Benny wouldn't let her go, maybe Rebecca would. After all, Rebecca loved her. Rebecca moved closer to Sarah and removed the duct tape. "Don't scream or you'll be dead. My cousin will come up and kill you."

"Rebecca please let me go. Untie me. You don't have to be like them. You're not a bad person. Please." Rebecca looked at her for a long time. She knew that this was wrong. She thought of all the other missing women. She knew that Benny had raped them. She knew that Rory had done the killing. She had seen all the tapes. This was not what she wanted for Sarah. She loved her. She had to let her go. It was the only way.

Rebecca began to untie Sarah's ropes. She went over to the closet and retrieved Sarah's nightgown. She handed it to Sarah. "Stay in this room. I don't think it is safe to go downstairs."

"Where is Beth?"

"I think that he has her in the basement. She's okay." Sarah felt major relief. Beth wasn't dead. Maybe there was a chance that they would make it out of here.

Sarah hugged Rebecca. "Thank-you." She watched Rebecca leave the room. Sarah pulled her nightgown over her head and ran to the door. She opened it slightly so that she could hear Rebecca. Maybe she would give her a sign. She waited with baited breath.

Rebecca went downstairs and saw her cousin sitting in his chair. He was painting more black roses. He stood up when he saw Rebecca. He thought that she had a suspicious look in her eyes. He wasn't sure if he could trust her. He was thinking she was going to squeal on him. "There's no need to paint anymore black roses. You already have her here." Rebecca said.

Rory went over to Rebecca and wrapped his strong hands around her neck. He began to strangle her. She kicked and thrashed at him. Her hands reached up to force his hands away from her. She couldn't breathe. She was surprised by his actions. She thought that he loved her. They were related for Christ sake. Why was he doing this to her? She couldn't free herself from his grasp. His hands tightened their grip and throttled her. Finally after a few more minutes of struggling, she slumped to the floor. She was dead. "Sinner," Rory shouted. She would be a prostitute no more. She was done.

Sarah couldn't hear anything. She stood there in silence. She wondered when Rebecca would come for her again. She hoped that Rebecca would shoot her cousin. Sarah looked around for a weapon. What if the killer came up instead of Rebecca. She had to be ready to save herself and find Beth. Could she get both of them out alive? She had to try. She waited longer. She didn't know what to do. She went to the window and looked outside. Suddenly she saw Douglass walking up to the house. He had found her. She waited by the door and listened for him.

Julie checked her email. She had received an email from the woman. Her name was Amy Black. Amy was asking to see her. Julie emailed her back and said that she would be right over. Julie changed into a revealing pink spandex shirt and a blue mini skirt. She put on black trouser socks and wore her black shoes. She grabbed her keys and stepped out of her house. She locked the door and got into her green car. She drove to Amy's house. She felt very excited. Maybe this was the moment that she was waiting for. She drove along and admired the sunny day. Maybe things were going to change for her. She wanted something new. It was like getting a sweet new computer. New things were great. She wanted Amy all to herself.

She arrived at Amy's house. She lived in a green cape house with hunter green shutters. Amy had a purple car in the driveway. Julie parked behind it and stepped out. She walked over to the porch and rang the doorbell. She felt a little nervous. She didn't know what was going to happen.

Amy opened the door and let her in. Amy had platinum blond hair that fell to her shoulders. It was thick and wavy. Big curls were in abundance. She had sapphire blue eyes and a heart shaped face. She had a mole on her cheek. Her eyebrows were thin and she was wearing blue eye shadow. She had lush red lips that badly needed kissing. She was wearing a form fitting green dress and black socks. She was tall and voluptuous. Her nose was straight, short and charming. "Hi, Julie. I've been waiting for this moment. Let's go sit on the couch." Amy led her to a floral sofa. Both sat down and locked eyes with each other. Their gaze intensified. Suddenly they both knew what was going to happen next. It was destined to happen. They had been emailing each other for several months. Both had written that they hated men. That was obvious. Both had been hinting about things.

"I've been wanting you so badly, Amy."

"Me too. I've been shy and was waiting for the right

moment to tell you of my feelings. I like you." Julie leaned over
and ever so softly touched Amy. Her lips trembled with sweet
desire as they brushed over Amy's lips. The delectable taste
was absolutely great. The tension between them began to melt.
Their kisses turned into intense flaming passion. The moment
at hand was lost in passion. Julie's hands slipped under Amy's
dress and she felt her thighs. Amy felt her body tingle at the soft,
gentle touch. Julie felt Amy's satin underwear and then felt the
delicious wetness of her vagina.

Amy pulled off Julie's pink shirt and discovered her black
lacy bra. Amy fumbled with the clasp and loosened the bra.
It cascaded to the floor and was abandoned in the heat of the
moment. Amy's lips began to suck at Julie's perky hard tits. Julie
moaned and cried out in ecstasy. "Oh, Amy. I love that." Amy
gently cupped Julie's breasts in her warm hands. Julie watched
as Amy slipped out of her dress. She wore a white jog bra. Amy
let Julie slip it over her head. Slowly and seductively, Julie's
gaze lowered to Amy's curvy body. Her naked form was pristine.
Amy's body ached for her touch. Julie's hands roamed over
Amy's body and she lowered herself to Amy's vagina. Her tongue
probed deep, deep and deeper into Amy's vagina. Amy climaxed
and cried out, "Ooh, baby! I'm coming!" Julie devoured her
delicious cream.

She leaned Amy against the couch and they bumped cunts
in the heated moment of swift passion. Gathering Amy into
her arms, Julie hugged her snugly. They kissed and brushed
each other's nipples and felt soft, elegant caresses. They made
love for several hours. They stopped to eat and then continued
to have sweet, passionate sex. Julie was completely happy. She
wanted to love Amy forever. Maybe they could adopt a baby
together. Julie's lips curved up in a satisfied smile. That was in
the future. Her world was new. For now, she craved sweet sex.
Amy was her vixen.

"Douglass knocked at the front door and rang the buzzer. The door opened and Rory stood in the doorway. He was wearing a plaid shirt and blue jeans. Douglass noticed his black hair. Suspect.

"I'm Detective Harrington. Can I come in and ask you some questions?"

"I suppose so." Rory let him into the mudroom. He didn't want him to go any further. Douglass looked at the white walls. He saw a red wooden chair by the door. A green trench coat was resting on it and below were a pair of L.L .Bean boots. Douglass saw the blood on one of the boots. He was thinking that now he had the right guy. He was staring into the eyes of the killer. Douglass tried to think fast and say what was on his mind. "I'm looking for a woman. Maybe you know her. Her name is Sarah Fisher." He showed Rory a picture of her. He looked at it for a moment and paused.

"No. I've never seen her."

"She's been missing since yesterday. Do you work at The Photo Shop?"

"Yes."

"Maybe you developed her films."

"I can't say that I have. I'm busy."

"Do you have a brother named Benny Jacobs?"

"No."

"Yes. You do. You lying sack of shit." Douglass walked towards the bureau that was against a wall. There was a mirror hanging against the wall. He looked into the mirror and got a bird's eye view of the living room. He saw the black roses on the coffee table and then he saw Rebecca's dead body on the floor. He pretended like he didn't see it. He felt himself trembling. He walked towards the door and hesitated. Then he turned around and tried to punch Rory in the face. He missed. Rory sent a horrific blow to his face. Douglass felt it smack his cheek so hard he thought he was seeing stars. Douglass sent an upper

cut to Rory's face and succeeded. Rory sent a severe punch to Douglass and hit him in the stomach. Douglass felt another blow to his nose and lips. He felt blood dripping down his face. Things were blurry for a moment until he tackled Rory to the floor. They had an all out fist fight that lasted at least ten minutes. Rory's hands grasped Douglass around the neck and tightened. At first Douglass couldn't breathe and felt himself turning blue or red in the face. Suddenly he had the strength to knock him off and he recharged his energy. Rory ran into the living room and Douglass tackled him again. They were fighting next to dead Rebecca. Now the cat was out of the bag. They fought for a little while longer. Finally Rory grabbed his gun and aimed it on Douglass. Douglass didn't know what to do. He was going to die and he wouldn't be able to help Sarah. Suddenly he saw Sarah standing in the doorway That led to the kitchen. She had tiptoed into the room. Douglass pretended as if he didn't see her. Suddenly she charged Rory and started attacking him. The gun went off and hit one of the walls. He dropped the gun and tried to get her off him. Then he grasped her neck and tried to strangle her. "Come any closer and she's dead." Sarah thought quick and sent a suffering blow to Rory's balls. He rolled over in agony and she got away. She grabbed the gun and aimed it at him.

"Move any closer to me and I'll shoot your nuts off, you sick bastard." Rory looked at Sarah and wondered if she would really do it. Then he was startled as the front door opened. In walked George. He went over to Rory and handcuffed him.

"Good work, Sarah. Rory Jacobs, you're under arrest for the murders of Teddy Barrington, Johnston Billings, Bernie Sanderson, Harold Baker, Susie Lockhart and Rebecca Simpson. I can't believe that you would kill your own cousin. She was your flesh and blood." George kicked him a few times to rough him up. "Larry is on his way."

Sarah dropped the gun and ran to Douglass. He held her

and hugged her. They kissed each other passionately. "It's all over. Thank-you for rescuing me." He said.

"Rebecca tried to save me. She untied me. She said that Beth is in the basement. She's alive."

Douglass found the door to the basement and went down. He opened the metal door and was shocked at what he saw. Beth was naked on the cot. He didn't want to know what the killer had done to her. "Hi, Beth. My name is Douglass Harrington. I'm a detective. Let's get your pajamas back on. Everything is over. The bad man is going to jail. He won't hurt you anymore. Aunt Sarah is waiting upstairs." Douglass helped her get dressed and then he carried her upstairs to Sarah.

She was seated on the couch. "Aunt Sarah! I thought I would never see you again." Beth rushed over to her and gave her a big hug. She kissed her cheeks.

"Honey, you're okay now. Did he hurt you?"

"He touched my private parts and made me touch him. It was gross."

"It wasn't your fault. He won't touch you anymore. You're safe now."

A few minutes later Larry came and pulled Rory to his feet. "Come on, asshole. You're going to prison where you belong. You sick bastard. You're going to get your just desserts. You've got it coming." Larry kicked him a few times and pulled him outside where he shoved him into the back of the squad car and locked the door. He drove him to the station. Later Rory would arrive at a larger prison to await his trial. He would be put away for a long time.

Douglass sat beside Sarah and Beth. Sarah called Judy to let her know that they had found Beth. She told Judy to meet them at the hospital. Douglass wanted to have Beth checked out to make sure that she wasn't harmed. He had a feeling that the killer had abused her. The two of them hopped into an ambulance about fifteen minutes later.

George and Douglass stayed in the house to check for evidence. George looked on a shelf near a big screen television. There were lots of DVDS. He picked one up and put it into the DVD player. After a minute it started playing. It showed Benny raping a woman. Then Rory came in later and strangled her. He put in several more DVDS and discovered the same thing with different women. "You were right. These must all be those missing women. Rory is also guilty of killing them. We can get Benny sent to jail for raping them. He'll go to jail for a long time."

George collected about twenty tapes and put them into a white garbage bag. It was all evidence. Douglass retrieved the 9mm gun. George called the forensics team to come over and pick up Rebecca. They waited for them to get there and then they headed over to Tangoes to bust Benny.

George and Douglass drove to Tangoes. They found Benny in his office. Benny was wearing a plaid shirt and blue jeans. "What's up, officers?" He looked at them with suspicious eyes.

"You're under arrest for rape charges to twenty two women. Twenty are dead and the other two are Sarah and Louisa. Your strip club is going under. Say good-bye to it."

"You can't do this. You don't have proof." George walked over and hand-cuffed Benny. He resisted and fought him. After a few minutes, George successfully had him cuffed.

"Your brother, Rory videotaped you. We've got twenty tapes that show you raped them. Your strippers are going to testify against you. You're going straight to jail, buddy." George forced him out of the club and shoved him into the back of the police car. He was going directly to jail. He was finished. Tangoes would be no more. The doors were locked.

Sarah and Beth were at the hospital. A few minutes later, Judy arrived and found Sarah and Beth. Judy quickly hugged her little girl and wouldn't let her go. She was so thankful that Beth was alive. "Did he hurt you?"

"He touched my private parts." *Judy was livid. She couldn't believe what she was hearing.*

"Oh my god. Well, it's over and he'll touch you no more. He's going to prison for a long time. You're safe now." *Judy hugged Beth some more. She thanked God that Beth was still alive.*

"I'm done stripping. Benny is going to jail. He raped me and a bunch of other women. I'm going to testify against him. It's time for me to find a regular job."

"Good. You don't need to sell your body to pay your bills. I'm glad that you're done."

"I met someone. He's a detective. His name is Douglass. He tried to save Beth and I. I think I helped save him. Rory had a gun pointing to him. I charged the killer and made him drop his gun."

"Wow. That must have been dangerous."

"Yes. At least it's over. I can move on with my life."

"That sounds great."

The three of them left the hospital and went home.

Sarah arrived home at her house and went upstairs to her bedroom. She held out a white kitchen trash bag and opened up her lingerie drawer. She grabbed all the edible underwear and threw them in the trash. She grabbed her skimpy thongs and threw them away too. She reached for a bunch of her stilettos and placed them in the bag too. She wasn't going to need to wear them anymore. She saved two pairs just in case she wanted to wear them. She grabbed her nurses uniform, the police uniform and several others that she would never wear again. She didn't want any reminders of her old life. She was throwing it away and would lock it forever in the past. It was a brand new moment for her.

She grabbed all her guns and planned on giving them to Douglass for safe keeping. The killer was locked up and she didn't have any need for protection. She would soon have her little puppy and he would be enough protection for her. She could hardly wait to collect Spunky. He was going to be a lot of fun.

She ate a frozen dinner with broccoli, chicken and linguine noodles. She had a can of Cherry Coke sitting on the end table. She picked up a most recent newspaper and started skimming the pages for job listings. There were a lot of different occupations to choose from. One jumped out at her. It was for a local florist shop. She thought about it and decided she would head there.

Later, she changed into a nice warm white sweater and a pair of dress slacks. She wore a pair of white flats and got in her car. She drove to about fifty places and filled out applications. About a week later she landed a job at the local florist shop called Fancy Flowers Florist Shop located in downtown South Haven. She started on a Monday. She was very lucky to land a fulltime job as the job market was hard to come by. She was excited about her new job. She thought that it would be lots of fun to work with lots of flowers. She loved the smell of them.

She worked during the day and had her evenings free to

see Douglass. Sarah thought of children. She could still have a child. Maybe she would finally be able to have babies. She had a big smile on her face as she thought of that prospect. Children of her own. How wonderful. Maybe there would someday be a little Lilly or Johnny in her life. She wanted to get to love a new baby.

Two weeks later Sarah was sitting on her porch in her wicker chair. She was wearing a blues shirt and a matching blue sweater. Her hair was in a ponytail. Her blue tie dyed skirt was down to her feet.

Douglass was sitting next to her. He was sipping coffee and doing the crosswords. He wore a yellow flannel shirt and blue jeans. At his feet was little Spunky. He was a golden retriever. He was busy chewing a big bone.

Douglass had moved in with Sarah. They were sharing the house and he was helping her pay off her credit cards. She was practicing staying away from the stores. She was being good about spending her money.

Sarah had a new job. She was a cashier at a florist shop. She was very happy with her new Job. She was very thankful that she didn't need to strip anymore. She just wondered why she hadn't made the change sooner.

She was very happy with Douglass. Douglass reached over and kissed her passionately. The flames of desire were ignited as they locked eyes together and embraced. Their bodies tingled as they touched each other. Caresses were soft and tender as they explored their new found love for each other. They sent fervent kisses to each other and tasted the wonderful flavor of the heated moment. They retreated to the bedroom and made wild, intimate love to each other. It was a whole new world for Sarah. The black roses were in the past and the killer brought to justice. She was free to love again. After all, love was what she dreamed of. She felt complete. Today was new and flames of desire soared. It was destiny.